BENJAMIN DRAGON
GENESIS

BENJAMIN DRAGON
GENESIS

Book 3 of The Chronicles of Benjamin Dragon

C. G. COOPER

Author: C. G. Cooper
Editors: Andrea Kerr & Cheryl Hopton

ISBN: 153772181X
ISBN-13: 9781537721811

Get a FREE copy of any C. G. Cooper novel just for subscribing at
>> http://CG-Cooper.com <<

To every person, young or old, who has ever been left on the sidelines, off the list or just on the fringe: know that you're never alone and that there is a place for you in this world.

CHAPTER 1

How is a 15-year-old supposed to save the world? I know it's an absurd question to ask. A mere five years ago, I never would have considered it, but now it's become my life's quest.

We're all in shock.

I watched the utter devastation unfold in my head (due to my special powers) while it was being broadcast on TV. *What a trip*. Cities from Tokyo to London were being destroyed and ravaged as Earth was trampled, assaulted by flying rocks and swallowed up whole by raging tsunamis.

Cities' populations were gone in the blink of an eye. Thousands were reported dead, then millions dead. Who was behind it? The Destructors - my enemy, my people. The ones who went wrong. We're the good side of those with gifts. They are the bad side.

I tried to convince myself that it was their fault—that it wasn't mine. That never worked. I was one of those kids who always took responsibility, whether I liked it or not. Maybe it's something my dad taught me or maybe it's how my mom raised me; I don't know. It was a hard thing to shake. Especially hard because I was only 15 years old. I felt like the world was exploding around me and I was somehow supposed to fix it. It seemed all I could do was cover my head and hope I wouldn't die.

The situation wasn't just about me, either. It involved my friends, as well as the other gifted ones. It included both my mom and dad. I was supposed to be responsible for saving them all. They'd been there for me at my side. They'd supported me with soothing words and there were loving hugs from my mother, but I always saw the hope in their eyes. That hope that I would do something more, that I would step out of my shell, even though I'd come so far. I wasn't the same ten-year-old kid who'd just found his gifts, the one scared of his own shadow half the time. I didn't cower anymore; I stood tall now. I was 15.

If the world were the same as it had been just five years ago, I'd be learning to drive. My life would revolve around the excitement of getting my driver's license and the near terror of asking a girl out on a date. But that world was long gone. We were living in a new reality – a reality I didn't want. The Destructors had changed it all. They'd taken that "normal" world from me; they'd taken it from all of us, gifted or not. *What was there to do*? We couldn't bandage up problems as cavernous as the Grand Canyon. How *do* you patch a hole the size of the Grand Canyon?

When you fly over Tokyo and see nothing but a caved-in mess, what can you do? There are no words to express the loss, the anger. How can you even begin to understand such an event, much less wrap your mind around it? Fifteen-year-old children aren't supposed to have to imagine—much less cope with—such devastation.

However, that's my life now, dealing with the unthinkable—the unimaginable. That's just my life, so I've got to deal with it. I have to suck it up and be a man. That's me—Benjamin Dragon—the 15-year-old man. I'd happily give up this new life and the role I find myself engulfed in, but that's just not going to happen anytime in the near future.

I stumbled out of my reverie, startled, trying to figure out where the voice was coming from. It sounded like it came from the bottom of a barrel. It took me a moment to remember my friends and I had slept in a cave again last night. Caves were all we ever slept in anymore. It felt like we were running, but from what and/or from whom? We weren't really running. We were searching.

Roy's voice came in, finally clear and very close. "Benjamin, are you ready to go?" His voice was low, fitting his huge frame. You'd never know he was also 15. He looked more like a 35-year-old bodybuilder who spent his life in gyms.

"Yeah, I'm almost ready," I said. "Give me a sec." Still crouching down after getting my attention, Roy looked at me, concerned. He was always there to protect me, hulking mass, deep friendship and all.

Roy had chiseled out the cave. It was one of his special talents. He used his gift, his telekinetic powers, to carve things. That was how he first figured out he had a gift. Back then, prior to all this chaos, he whittled horses' heads and bears out of chunks of oak, cedar and pine, without any tools. Now, he shaped the earth to help us survive. He'd sculpted this cave out of a cliff face overlooking the California Coast.

There we were, hanging off the edge of a cliff, in a cave, hiding like rats. I hated the feeling. The cave was dark and damp. Even the pleasant smell of fresh kelp wafting up to us from the ocean couldn't change the fact we were hiding out, like vagabonds, in a cave. For morale, we had to get out of here soon; although we'd only spent a night, it felt like ages since we arrived. Time's a funny thing when you're not sure whether you want it to slow down or speed up.

"Come on. Let's go," I said, standing quickly and moving to the entrance. When I got outside, I saw that Roy had done a little bit more to carve out the ledge overlooking the Pacific Ocean.

Xander, another friend, was leaning against one of the outer walls, his long hair partially covering his eyes. He was flipping something in the air. At first I couldn't make out what it was. I walked over to him; then I froze. It was a dirty baby doll. I knew where he'd gotten it: from the last crisis site.

"Throw it away," I demanded.

"What?" he looked up, finally realizing I was there.

"I said throw it away." That's when he realized what he'd done. Xander showed no remorse; he never did. That's just the way Xander was. But he did as he was told and let go of the spinning baby doll; we watched as it tumbled down, finally splashing into the ocean. That doll was a reminder of all those dead—children and whole families gone. I couldn't bear to see that reminder of so much death and destruction. Xander knew better than to bring along souvenirs. We had all agreed. He might not like the fact that I was the leader of our group, but I was. His had been the one deciding vote, five years ago, that determined my role.

When the voting was done, not many people had wanted a ten-year-old kid in charge, but what could the others say? I was the only one who had all three gifts: telekinesis, growing and healing, while the others only had one. Xander helped put me in charge. Now, he would play along. He was good like that. I could never hate him. He was my brother after all. Not my real brother; we'd been through a lot together. Just like real brothers, we fought sometimes. At times, the anger went both ways. But heck, he'd saved me and I'd saved him, so we were brothers until the end. But he still had a way of just getting to me. That spinning baby doll....

The twins, Jasmine and Lily, stood up from where they'd been whispering to each other. That's what they'd always done since I met them. Even though they were 15 as well, they still copied each other's clothing and actions, similar to when they were five-years-old.

"Are you okay?" Lily asked me.

"Yeah, I'm fine. Thanks," I said. "You guys ready to go?" Everyone nodded.

"Where to now?" Xander asked, standing up and doing a flip in midair just for the hell of it. Xander was the show-off of the bunch and that was one of the reasons he got under my skin sometimes. I ignored his little flip and talked to the girls and Roy instead. "I thought maybe we'd go down to the beach, spend a little time soaking up some sun," I said.

They all looked at me like I was crazy. We'd been flying from city to city (without the use of aircraft), for what felt like an eternity, which is darned tiring. We were all exhausted so I thought a bit of rest and relaxation would do us some good. I guess one mark of a good leader is knowing when your troops need a rest. I was trying to be that good leader.

"Yeah, that's a great idea," Roy said.

"Shoot, maybe we'll meet some girls down there," Xander remarked. He loved talking about girls; in fact, it was his favorite subject. I guess his hormones were kicking into overdrive.

We chose a place called the Lucia Lodge for lunch. We were dressed in hiking gear so we fit right in. We only had to hide our flying helmets on the way in. Since we weren't riding motorcycles, we might have looked a little funny walking in with helmets under our arms. Of course, they might have thought we were out mountain biking, but why take the chance? Anyway, we settled in at a nice table on the little outdoor patio overlooking the Pacific Ocean. It was pretty, and the view almost got my mind off things. We ordered lunch. I ordered a Reuben with fries; it sounded really good. Roy ordered two sandwiches like he always did. Xander asked for the biggest sandwich on the menu after his attempt to get a burger failed. The twins always got salads; today was no exception.

We were sitting there (I was almost relaxed), looking around and drinking in the view, watching the birds swoop down over the ocean, when somebody turned on a TV at one side of the patio. I hadn't even noticed it when we walked in. Honestly, I never watched TV any more. All people seemed to watch these days was the news, whether to find out about the newest catastrophe, or just to watch the chaos unfold before them. What made people so interested in watching other peoples' misfortunes? People get called looky-loos when they pause to check out an accident while they're driving, but no one seems to say anything about the people who get hung up on television news. It was morbid, the way they flocked to watch. For years, people had stayed glued to the television set—only watching news. Some people thought it got old, but inexplicably, every time there was a new catastrophe, there was a *Breaking News Alert* and people would flock to the television like moths to a flame.

They were talking about the latest catastrophe, somewhere in China. I didn't recognize the locale. I tried tuning it out by talking to Roy, but he was only half listening, his attention on the television.

Xander piped up, "Hey, I'll bet you five bucks they're gonna have Jacee on. Any takers?" Nobody took him up on his bet; it was a given Jacee would be televised. I reluctantly turned my attention to the newscast.

The reporter was on scene in China, and the place was a total disaster. There was jagged rubble everywhere. There were all kinds of smoke, but it did nothing to hide the pure chaos. Unfortunately, we had seen this what seemed like hundreds of times before. You never really got used to the complete disaster. A triage area had been established with tents and helpers rushing to and fro. Then there were the wounded with bloody bandages lying in the open, and the dead covered in discolored sheets. There was no more room for them in the tents.

Just as Xander predicted, a couple minutes after the broadcaster started talking, the cameraman zoomed in on the scene. A close-up showed the reporter along with Jacee Trevane, my nemesis. To most of the world's people, he was an all-around awesome guy. He was a former pop star, actor and global entertainer. Now, he was the face of the relief efforts for all the destruction going on around the globe. The funny thing was—okay, not so funny—people were completely unaware that Jacee was causing all this destruction. He was becoming even more famous than before for providing relief efforts for the massive devastation, but he was the one who caused it all.

He was leading The Destructors in taking over what used to be our world. Now he was leading the effort, the underground effort, to take over everything. To take all the power with no caring about what got broken or who was injured or killed. There he was, with that mournful face, playing it up like he always did. He even had some streaks of dirt on his face as he distributed bottles of water and patted a woman on the hand. He pretended to avoid the reporter, trying to make it look like he wasn't paying attention to anything but the victims.

Our little group knew the truth. Jacee was always aware of the cameras and it was a choreography I'd seen countless times. But, if you didn't know what you were looking for, you would only see that he was just another famous guy, providing his fame to get others to assist in the disaster relief.

The reporter turned to face Jacee. "Mr. Trevane, could you tell us what the situation is on the ground?"

Jacee looked up as if he'd just realized the reporter was there. Then he glanced into the camera briefly, and back to the child who was taking a water bottle from his hand. "It's not good; I'm not going to sugarcoat it," Jacee said, "There are a lot of people hurting, a lot of people dead. As you can see, there is complete and utter devastation. We just pushed the world too far. Global warming: nobody wanted to listen to the facts. Nobody wanted to listen to the warnings and now look at us."

He held his hands wide now, looking all around like he was preaching to someone. He continued, "I don't know what else to say. We've traveled all around the world trying to help these unfortunate people—trying to put their lives back together. But how do you rebuild from this? I just don't know." Then he looked straight into the camera as he pleaded, "If there's anything you can do or anything you can give to the Red Cross or to my foundation, Trevane International, please help us. We can't bring in supplies fast enough. We need money to help people rebuild and to buy supplies to keep them alive. Please help if you have money; I encourage you to help us. We need your help, not just here but worldwide. It's the right thing to do. That's all I have for right now."

The reporter turned back to the camera. "As you can see, the situation is dire. Mr. Trevane is doing his best, but I will echo his words in saying he needs your help. We all need your help. Please, will you help us?"

I tore my attention from the television, away from Jacee's grandstanding. Thoughts of Jacee being the cause of the mayhem and then profiting from it, turned my stomach. By now the newscaster was babbling about something else. I got up from the table, left the porch and headed down for a closer view of the ocean. There were some picnic tables lower down with a better view. I had lost my appetite.

I thought about what I'd seen over and over again. Jacee Trevane was the face of it all. The two-sided, black-and-white, yin and yang all wrapped into one evil mastermind. He was no good. He had tried to recruit me; at one point, he had attempted to recruit all of us. Now he was trying to convert the rest of humanity to his way of thinking. Global warming had nothing to do with it, but we still didn't know exactly what was causing all the destruction.

It would take, we had estimated, hundreds of The Destructors, all put together, to cause this level of utter devastation, and yet we couldn't find them. We'd found one or two, here or there. We'd brought most of them into custody, but some we'd had to fight to the death. We'd lost some people on our side. Too many really, but we hadn't found the hundreds of Destructors we were looking for. It was like they were hidden or covered with a cloaking spell, not wanting to be found. We'd done everything we could. It wasn't enough.

I was supposed to be the one that could find them using my additional gifts. That was a joke. I had visions. I could see things, but this ability wasn't helping me one bit right now. I walked down to the face of the cliff, thinking I should just jump off and fly away, leaving my friends behind. It might be for a short time—just to gain some perspective, or a little clarity—maybe just for a bit. I wanted so much to step off and rocket into the air leaving all our problems behind, but I stopped. I would not be able to forget about the world, and as I looked down, I knew I couldn't afford to escape right now.

Then I heard it. Well, I shouldn't say I heard it. It's hard to explain it—I saw it, heard it, or maybe both. I didn't really know. There it was in the back of my head. It was like a whisper, kind of a rasp, like a skeleton coming out of a closet, "Help." I froze. I looked all around; there was nobody near me. Then I heard it again: "Help." Still no one.

Don't ask me how—because I have no idea—but in that moment, the second time I heard that plea, I knew that whoever or whatever was behind that voice was behind the destruction of half the world.

CHAPTER 2

I don't know how long I stood there. I kept listening in my head. The voice was gone, but I rewound it, trying to identify who the voice belonged to. There had been no distinct tone, inflection, background sounds, or any other hint to provide me a clue. Nothing reminded me of anyone I knew. The voice was pleading and, at the same time, it sounded tired. Like somebody just waking up from a nap and calling for help, but not knowing exactly where they were or who could help them.

I don't know how long I stood there. Before I knew it, the others had joined me. They were there standing right next to me, like always. Roy stood the closest, looking me up and down. "Are you okay?" he asked, alarmed. I nodded, even though I felt far from alright. "You saw something," Roy said.

I looked up at him. His face was gripped with apprehension. He was always concerned about me. He took the role of being my protector quite seriously. While I loved it sometimes and cherished him for even being there with me, other times it kind of freaked me out. No, it didn't really creep me out. That was the voice. The way it had called out to me. Like it was calling straight to me. It was not just an empty message sent out for just anyone to hear. It was if the person behind the voice had picked up on a direct line to me pleading, "Benjamin, help me. Benjamin, help me!"

"I'm fine," I lied. "Did you save my lunch?"

Xander held up a plastic bag that had a Styrofoam package in it. "I've got it right here," he pronounced, "I only took a couple bites."

I smiled. "I know I said we should spend some time relaxing at the beach, but now I think we should get going."

They all looked at me; I saw in their faces a mixed bag of disbelief and dashed hopes, as well as understanding. There was a little disappointment in Xander's eyes, but he didn't say anything. He could tell when something was up. Even he knew when to keep his mouth shut. I didn't say anything further.

Roy asked, "Do you think we should go home, back to Italy?" I didn't know, honestly. Every part of me wanted to go home to see my mom and dad, back to our safe little—well, huge—mansion on the side of Lake Como. It was my home, but then I guess it was everyone else's home, too.

We spent more time on the road than we did there, but heck, it was safe. It was where we could finally completely relax, be ourselves and not try to be who we weren't—or at least who we didn't feel like we were. See, in the blink of an eye, we had become 15-year-old adults. People had put their lives in our hands. We traveled the world helping and recruiting. In fact, that's what brought us to California: we were looking for more of our kind.

"I think we should go. I think we should leave right now," I emphasized.

Everyone nodded. Lily and Jasmine held each other's hands. They were fifteen, but still so doll-like. It was something we'd become accustomed to. It was how they were; they were extremely close. It must be nice to have family nearby at all times to share the good and the bad. I don't recall ever seeing them apart.

I closed my eyes, trying to focus. There it was like a flickering flame, far to the south. I had the mental picture. Without opening up my eyes I said, "Okay. I've got it. He's still there."

When I opened my eyes, everybody was already in prep mode. We'd have to walk back to retrieve our helmets, but that wouldn't take long. What I really wanted was to be back in the air again where I felt free. Flying was when I felt most like myself.

So off we flew on yet another leg of our adventure in our ongoing quest to find more gifted individuals to assist us in our cause. We needed all the help we could get to discover the answers we were searching for so desperately. I didn't know if we'd find anything in what was left of Los Angeles, but we had to try. It was the only thing we could do. People were counting on us, and at least maybe we could help one kid who was sitting there wondering why, all of a sudden, he could move things using his thoughts.

I don't know why, and I'm not sure if it was just luck or if somebody like Jacee Trevane had actually planned it this way, but the undamaged area of Los Angeles was the most affluent section of the city. A place called Pacific Palisades, in part of what remained of Santa Monica, was still pretty. It looked untouched by the ruination surrounding it. It also overlooked what remained of the vast Los Angeles landscape.

Flying into the area was weird. I'd been to Los Angeles before, but I hadn't been back since it had been destroyed. We took our time when we touched down not far from the Riviera Country Club where I knew the gifted child we'd been seeking was living.

Xander kept jabbering on and on about the houses. "Jeez, can you believe people still live in places like this? Can you believe places like this still exist?"

All of us kept walking. I guess you could say that we were pretty well off too. We could fly all around the world and had plenty of resources at our disposal. We could go almost anywhere and do almost whatever we wanted. We had plenty of money. I don't know exactly how much. My family made sure we'd be ok financially. It wasn't such a bad life, if you could block out what was happening in the world, but Xander was right. Street after street lined with huge houses and pristine lawns, like life here was a bubble, left unscathed, while the rest of the world seemed to be falling in on itself.

I tried to ignore it, but even I couldn't help staring at the green grass, tall walls and the ladies walking their long-legged dogs down the streets. They pretty much ignored us. We just looked like any other bunch of kids walking down the street.

It was a different story when we reached the gate of the country club. A paunchy guard stepped out of the shack wearing a Riviera Country Club shirt and demanded to know what we wanted. As usual, Roy took the lead. "Sir," he said. "we're here to visit a friend." The guard looked at him like he was being pranked. Then he looked at each of us, giving us the old once-over. He looked back at Roy—or rather, looked up at him. Roy is pretty tall.

"And who would your friend be?" the guard asked. Roy didn't flinch.

"Francis Stapleton," I said. The name appeared in my head in a nanosecond, even though I hadn't known his name a moment before.

The guard looked at me dubiously. "And how do you know Mr. Stapleton?" he asked.

"He's a friend of ours," I said. "Now can we go see him?"

The guard gave us one more look. "I'll have to make a call," he said.

I nodded, like it didn't matter whether we gained entrance. Inside I was worried that maybe we wouldn't get in. I was afraid this one time we wouldn't get past the guard—not that there ever had been guards before. Usually we found gifted kids in somebody's house, a refugee camp or something like that. This was a country club, but he came back a minute later and announced, "You can go in." He pressed a button and the metal gates swung open, slowly, like they were as hesitant as the guard to let us inside.

We walked into the country club estate. It was even more amazing than the streets beyond its walls. There were expensive cars lined up like it was some kind of bank vault for the rich. Maseratis, Lamborghinis, Ferraris, Audis. I shouldn't say Audis, because that was the cheapest kind they had there. Porsches, Bentleys, Rolls Royces. You name it, they had it. They lined the streets and parking lots. It was similar to gilding furniture: the cars added the bling to the country club. We were all wide-eyed and slack jawed as we walked. I'm surprised we didn't trip on our tongues or slip on our drool. Even Roy, who was the least materialistic of our bunch, couldn't help but look around like we had somehow entered an alternate reality. When we finally made it to the end of the circular drive, we entered the lobby.

As soon as we walked in, we felt completely out of place. We were kind of dirty, wearing scuffed clothes and our hair was mussed up from our flight down. When the guy at the front register looked at us, I thought there might be a problem, but there wasn't. He looked us up and down and then he flashed his nicest smile.

"You must be here for Mr. Stapleton," he said. I nodded. "Will you please follow me?" He took us to a back stairwell, which felt more like a secret hallway. It was weird. As soon as we closed that door, it was as if we had stepped back in time. For a moment, I felt like Alice stepping through the looking glass. The smells were completely different from those of the lobby. It smelled of varnished wood and ancient carpet. It wasn't disgusting or anything. It did feel like we were stepping into a grandparent's house or maybe a house from the 1920s. It was almost comforting. You know what it smelled like? It smelled like money.

As we went up to the second level, I surveyed all the old pictures and knickknacks in glass cases. Lots of golf memorabilia took up the most room. It was like time stood still there, unchanged and perfectly preserved. Lights, air conditioning, etc. were still functioning. The Destructors hadn't touched this place. We walked down the hallway once we finally reached the second floor. Some of the rooms were marked with brass plates. One door plaque had Walt Disney etched into bronze. There was another one that said Dean Martin. We passed more pictures and encountered more funny smells. I could see Roy drinking in all the details as if he'd never been in a place like this. He came from a rural background, so I couldn't blame him. Even I was kind of staring at things with wonder. It was so plush compared to our place on Lake Como, we were all kind of overwhelmed.

We passed a room that was being cleaned and it had pretty much the same décor as the remainder of the hallway. Inside were some antiques. There was a hint of modern times: a flat screen TV, like a picture, on the wall. I expected pretty much the same thing when we arrived at Francis's room. Francis is a strange name. Maybe he'd be as strange as his name. No offense to any Francises out there, but most of the ones I'd met went by Frank.

When we reached the room, the desk clerk knocked. Somebody called from inside. The door was opened by a woman; it wasn't Francis. "May I help you?" she asked.

"Mr. Stapleton's guests have arrived," the man from the front desk said.

I saw the woman peer out and look at us. She was an older woman. I didn't know if maybe it was Francis's grandmother or mother, or maybe she worked for him.

"Let them in, woman," barked a voice from within. Kind of nasally and, I don't know, maybe what I would consider Californian. What a weird combination. The woman looked annoyed but moved aside, opening the door, and let us pass her. When we stepped inside, the room had a completely different décor from what we'd seen in the hallway and the room being cleaned. All the furnishings were modern. There was a bank of five flat screen TVs almost covering one wall.

Across from the televisions was a scrawny little kid sitting in a wheelchair. His head looked too big for his body and he had super thick glasses. He didn't even look up to greet us, keeping his eyes trained on the screens and concentrating on the video game he was playing. "That's all now," he said, dismissing the woman. She disappeared with the man from the front desk.

"You're here to see me," he announced, without looking away from his video game where he was shooting moaning zombies.

"Yeah, we were wondering if you had a few minutes to talk," I said. Every other newly gifted kid that I'd met had responded to our appearance with humility. They usually acted scared or at least curious. But not this kid, Francis Stapleton. I don't know—I couldn't put my finger on it. There was something different about him. Like he felt that he owned the world or maybe, due to his handicap, the world owed him? He gave off a snotty attitude that really rubbed me the wrong way. I tried to push the thoughts aside, trying to keep an open mind, but honestly, by this time, my brain was already frazzled. I was in no mood for his arrogance or sense of entitlement.

"What did you want to talk to me about?" he asked with an impatient tone.

"Do you mind turning off the game?" I asked. "This is kind of important,"

Roy stepped around me and turned off each one of the televisions. The kid looked annoyed and even huffed, but when he looked up at Roy, he hushed, for a moment.

He swiveled in his wheelchair and I could see his body better. His skin was wrinkled and his body looked shriveled like a prune. An overwhelming sense of empathy rose in me all of a sudden. I mean, what could happen to a kid to put him in a wheelchair like that? But then his snarky face snarled, "That wasn't very nice."

I really didn't like this kid. "Hey, look. We're here to help. If you want to listen to us, cool. If not, we can go." He took a minute to decide. I could hear Xander in the background tapping his foot. He was ready to go. Jasmine and Lily were quiet, as usual.

Finally, he spoke up, "Okay, what did you want to see me about?"

"It's about your gifts," I said. Now one of his eyebrows raised.

"What about my gifts? What about them?"

"We know you have them and we want to help," I said.

"You want to help me?" he laughed. "I think we should be talking about how I could be helping you."

I gave Roy a quizzical look which I extended to Xander and the twins. We were all incredulous. How could he help us? We'd been wrong before, but honestly, the five of us were in no mood to hear this.

I exhaled. "Look, we're gifted too, and we're just here to see if you need our help."

Truthfully, we were there to recruit him. We needed every gifted person we could get, and my senses were screaming that he was a Destructor. We could use every one that we could recruit to help in our crusade. Technically, we weren't called The Destructors now that we had renamed ourselves. We needed more power on our side, the side of The Keepers.

"Look, you can move things, right? Like with your mind? Do things? And it's something that just came into being for you?" He looked at me. I couldn't read what he was thinking.

And I was usually pretty good at that. Was he playing Jedi mind tricks? Francis was pretty good at commanding the room; he was used to getting his own way. That I could see. He looked at me with—what's the word? Not contempt but boredom or patronizing patience.

"Look, guys," he said. "I've had this gift, as you call it, for as long as I can remember."

Wait a minute, what was he saying? "How old are you?" I asked.

"I'm twelve," he said.

"When did you first know you were...different?"

He chuckled. "Different? I've always been different. Look at my body, man. Look at me. I've been in a wheelchair forever. You know how to walk. I can't walk, but that's how long I've had my gift."

How could that be? Everybody I'd ever met that had a gift had received it when they were ten years old. Maybe something was changing again. What kind of implications did that leave for the rest of us?

"So you're saying that you've had your gifts ever since you can remember?"

"Well, not exactly," he wavered. "I'd say it probably started five years ago. Like, when everything else started happening."

That made more sense.

"What do your parents think?" I asked. Something flicked and flashed in his eyes, but then it disappeared.

"My parents are dead," he stated.

"I'm sorry," I replied, genuinely contrite. I couldn't imagine losing my parents.

"It's okay. They died when L.A. went up in flames. They were at some benefit brunch while I was in physical therapy.

Not that the therapy helped me, but yeah. That happened and now here I am."

Francis really was different. He'd been left alone. It looked like he had some money, but that still didn't explain why he'd had his gifts for longer than most of us. I mean, I'd found out about mine at age ten and so had the rest of my team: Roy, Xander, Jasmine and Lily. In fact, Jasmine and Lily were originally from Los Angeles. Their dad had gotten out of Los Angeles just in the nick of time, right before all the destruction started.

"Anyway," I said. "We're here to see if first, you need our assistance, and second, if you would like to join us."

He looked at me funny. "You mean you guys are like The Avengers or something? Or is this like the new superhero thing? Is that what you guys do?" he asked, sarcasm coating each word.

I exhaled again. It was hard to explain to some people. Well, not most people. Most gifted kids got it, but not this Francis kid. Man. Yeah, it must stink to lose your parents, but it didn't mean you had to be a complete clown box.

"Look, the stuff that's been going on in the world—it's not what you think."

Now his eyes went wide. "Are you saying you guys are behind all this?" he asked.

"Look, I can't really tell you what's going on. All I can say is if you come with us, we can provide you with some of the answers you're looking for."

"Why should I come with you?" he inquired. "I'm pretty happy here. I've got plenty of money. I can do basically whatever I want. Why should I come with you guys? Sounds like a whole lot of bull."

I didn't know how I was going to deal with this guy. Usually it was pretty easy. It was either a "yes" or a "no", but this time it was all wrong. I just wasn't getting a good vibe from him at all.

"Look, I can leave you a card with a phone number to call. If you want to join us, give us a shout. If not, no big deal. But we're always around if you need help."

He laughed again. I really didn't like this kid. No matter if he lost his parents or if he was stuck in a wheelchair; it didn't mean I had to be nice to him.

"Let's go guys," I said, turning back to my friends. "We've got some place to be." Everyone filed out of the room; all I could think about was what Francis would decide.

Francis turned on the TV again. Just one monitor this time, back to the game he had been playing, but he didn't click it off pause. He just watched the screen for a minute, thinking. Then he picked up the cell phone that was on the table next to him and dialed a number from memory.

"Francis?"

"Yeah, it's me," Francis answered.

"What do you need?"

"I just had a visit from the group you were telling me about," Francis said. "They're trying to recruit me like you said."

"What did you tell them?"

"I didn't tell them anything," Francis declared. "You told me not to."

"Good, good. Well, take a little time. Don't appear too anxious. Then give them a call and tell them you're in."

"What do you want me to do after that?" Francis asked. "I've got a lot of things to do here."

"Do you, or don't you, want to be part of this? You told me you did."

"Well, of course, but—"

"There's no but. You make a decision; you're either with me or you're not. You want a place with me, you got it. If you don't, tell me now."

For the first time, Francis felt flustered. Well, not exactly flustered, but very nervous. Jacee Trevane wasn't someone you trifled with. Jacee Trevane was—well—Jacee Trevane. He was the man of the hour right now. The whole world knew who he was and looked to him for leadership. If he, Francis Stapleton, could attach himself to Jacee Trevane and become part of his crew—well, all the money in the world couldn't buy him a place next to that type of power.

"Okay," Francis said. "I'm in. I'll let you know when I tell them."

CHAPTER 3

The guy from the front desk was waiting for us when we left Francis's room. After letting him know we wouldn't be leaving yet, but needed a place to talk, he suggested holding our meeting in the tennis lounge: down a couple flights of stairs, outside, overlooking the tennis courts. The location just happened to be removed from the hallowed halls of the main building, and I suspected he'd suggested the place because of how we were dressed. We weren't exactly decked out per country club code. Everyone else was dressed in suits, khakis or golf gear. I didn't even see anybody talking on their cell phones.

The tennis lounge was comfortable, so we took seats, ordered some food and waited to see if Francis would call.

"I really think we should get out of here, guys. I mean that Francis kid is kind of a creep, and I don't mean to be mean, but he's kind of weird looking," Xander said.

Nobody disagreed. I didn't like Francis's attitude but we'd been sent to California to recruit kids with special powers, not for winners of congeniality awards. So far the recruiting hadn't gone well. We'd had three people decline, and Francis was the fourth tallied on my mental list.

"I think we should wait," I said. "He's the last one that I've got, at least for now."

"What if you come up with another one?" Jasmine asked. They all knew that my "gifts" were a little spotty sometimes. Sometimes it was like a person tweaked my antenna and the picture was perfect; other times the only picture I got was useless – just static. I mean I was supposed to have this crazy clarity but that happened so rarely now that I was wondering if I was losing my mental capacity.

"Yeah," Lily said in agreement, "maybe if we hang around you'll come up with something or we'll find someone else."

I didn't know what to say. I wanted to go home; I wanted to see my parents. Not to mention that I desperately needed a good night's sleep. Restful nights had been tough to come by lately. The dreams didn't help, but mostly I just couldn't relax, even though I was surrounded by my best friends in the world.

What did that say about me? What did that say about what we were doing? *What did that say about our future?* I mean I was supposed to be one of the people responsible for saving the world. Come on, really?

It was Roy who made the ultimate decision, relieving me of the duty. "We should stay," he said. "We should give Francis the opportunity to join if he wants to. It took each of us a little time to wrap our heads around the initial offer."

I agreed and, with much reluctance, Xander did as well. However, he seemed distracted. I don't know, he was usually in pretty good spirits, at least for what could be expected from Xander. He was one of my best friends, but I can say he didn't always have the best attitude. That's cool—everybody's different; I'm not chipper all the time, especially after all that's happened. There was something just beneath Xander's surface that I couldn't place, and I wished I could read his mind.

I didn't have a chance to ask Xander if something was bothering him then: our food was delivered and we started to devour it. We chatted about this and that as we ate. For the most part, Jasmine and Lily bantered with each other. They seemed to always have something to say, and Roy listened with great interest. Not for the first time, I caught him staring at Lily, not in a weird way, just different. I didn't know if there was anything to it. I liked them both, and I wasn't jealous. I was happy for Roy if that's what he wanted, but I hadn't seen Lily reciprocate his interest.

Roy is probably my best friend on the earth, and I didn't want to see him get hurt, so I kind of said a silent prayer that maybe Lily would come around and share his feelings. I was just getting up to throw away my trash when I froze. I heard it again.

"Help! Help!" It was more urgent this time, like the person that I'd heard before was waking up, and that in some way, their mind wasn't as jumbled as it was earlier. Blocking out the conversations around me, I tried to listen so I might be able to pinpoint where it was coming from. Just like I do when I find the newly gifted.

"Help!" I heard one last time. I didn't know, again, how long I had been standing there.

"Are you okay?" Lily asked.

I shook my head and looked at her. "Yeah, I'm fine."

"You don't look fine," she said. "You were, like, totally zoned out."

I gave her a sheepish grin and said, "You know me and my crazy brain. Sometimes I zone out." I could tell she didn't believe me. Lily and Jasmine had a way of looking into your soul and seeing if you were telling the truth, especially Lily.

It's one of the reasons I enjoyed their company. They were kind of our truth/BS detectors. I wasn't always good at it, even though I was better than most. But Lily and Jasmine—I don't know—it's like the way they somehow knew with one hundred percent accuracy what you had in your pocket. Whether it was a set of keys, a wallet or a pebble—they just knew. They had this intuitive ability to look into things that other people couldn't see.

"Seriously, I'm fine," I said. "I was just thinking about stuff."

"Were you thinking about your parents?" Lily asked.

Roy walked over, his face scrunched with concern. "What's going on?"

"Benjamin is acting…weird," Lily said.

Roy looked down at her, "Like more than usual?" That actually made Lily laugh. This time I saw something different in her face, like she was relaxing. Something about—about the way she regarded Roy.

"I don't know. Maybe I'm wrong," she said. "Come on, let's go. Looks like this kid just isn't going to call."

We took the long way back to the front of the country club. There was the pristine putting green. Then on the tee box, a foursome of middle-aged men, in near-matching golf outfits, were tossing a coin to see who would tee off first. The tennis courts were next, almost half filled with women in short skirts and fashionable tops. People playing golf and tennis, like they had no cares in the world. Not even a mile away, there was a huge hole in the ground. There it looked like the Earth had pressed a button making most of Los Angeles disappear into some sort of massive sinkhole. I mean it was crazy, right? People didn't seem to care or else had become so accustomed to it, they could keep playing their favorite sport at some ritzy country club. Instead of hitting overheads on tennis courts, maybe they could have more empathy for those less fortunate. They could be doing something to help others. Then again, what else should they do? Life didn't stop just because of unfortunate circumstances, especially when it was someone else's circumstances.

As we walked past the eighteenth hole, I had an epiphany. I realized that was what I'd been doing. I had stopped living my real life. I had put everything on hold as if saving the world was *my job* now. It was exhausting and there were days I pretended like everything was cool. I pretended to be okay, but I really wasn't. As we approached the guard shack, it occurred to me that I'd forgotten how to live life. Everything happening around me had also swallowed up every piece of what had been Benjamin Dragon. I had also become a victim of the massive sinkholes around the world.

I no longer savored the taste of food or took time to enjoy playing video games. I used to love books, losing myself in them for hours. But I hadn't read a book in months and that wasn't me. I had become a fifty-year-old man squirreled away in the body of a fifteen-year-old. I didn't like it. It just made me—I don't know—it made me think that there had to be something more. Think about all those heroes in centuries past—they couldn't just worry about their job and helping others all the time. They had to be selfish sometimes in order to help others. It was like on airplanes when they said to put on your own oxygen mask first, then help others. I knew it was important for each of us to take care of ourselves, but I hadn't been able to justify that for any of us, especially me, not in the face of all the devastation.

I don't know where I was going with what I was thinking. I promised myself that I would talk to my dad about all of it as soon as we got back to Italy. Maybe he would have an idea; he always seemed to be the one who had achieved the right balance. Even when he was working long hours, he found time to play with me, take mom on dates or play a round of golf. He was the athletic one in the family. *Yeah, that's it. Dad would know the answer.* We were close and I could ask him questions like that. I'd just made up my mind about what I was going to ask dad when the phone in my pocket rang. I looked at the number; it had to be Francis.

"Hello," I answered.

"Uh, yeah. Hey, it's Francis."

"Oh. Hi, Francis."

"Um, so yeah, I was wondering. If the offer still stands, I would like to come with you guys."

"Oh, that's great," I said, not really meaning it, not really sure I wanted him with us. But after all, it was our job. "So, should we come back to get you?" I asked.

"Yeah, let me get a couple things together, but," he paused, "would it be okay if we went on a little detour before we go to wherever it is you're going to be taking me?"

"Um, sure, I guess. What did you have in mind?"

"I know this might sound weird, but I've got some property in Northern California, in Monterey. Do you know where that is?"

Yeah, I knew where that was. "Sure. We were up there not too long ago."

"Oh. Okay, great. When we get up there, I've got to settle some things before we can go. You know without my parents around I'm kind of the man of the house. You know what I mean?" he asked.

I did. I knew exactly what he meant. I had been the "man of the house," for a few years now. Only it wasn't just for our home, it was for our community of the gifted: The Keepers.

Maybe we did have some things in common, even though my parents weren't gone, but sometimes—Well, I won't get into that right now. "Okay, we'll come back to get you and then we'll take off."

"Okay. I'll see you in a few minutes."

I hung up the phone and looked at my team. "Well, it looks like he's in."

Lily gave me a smile, Jasmine looked reserved as usual, Xander huffed and Roy just nodded. That was Roy, always stoic. Roy, my protector, was the one who always kept us going. He was the glue binding us all together. He was always reminding us that we had a job to do. Not that I couldn't stay on task, but, well, it kind of helps to have somebody around to keep you in line.

"Why don't you guys go back to get him while I make a quick call?" They headed toward the lobby and I dialed my dad's phone number.

He picked up after a couple rings. "Hey buddy, how are you doing?" he asked. His voice sounded cheery, but I could sense that there was something else there.

"Hey Dad, I just wanted to check in and tell you that hopefully we're going to be heading your way soon."

"Oh, okay. Well yeah, things are going okay here." It wasn't like Dad to stall; we were honest with each other. Honesty first and always—that's what he'd always told me. That's just the way we were.

"Do you mind if I talk to Mom? Is she around?"

Dad didn't answer.

I heard, more than felt, my heart *thud*.

"She's—um—she's not here right now, buddy. Um, I'll tell her that you called, okay?"

"Dad, what's going on?"

He didn't say anything for a long moment. "Buddy, Mom had to go. She, well, she wasn't feeling well again, and, you know, she's got to go see the experts so they can help her. She didn't really want you to be around while she was going through that stuff."

Mom had been dealing with some scary mental issues for a while. It all went back to when she'd been captured by The Destructors. Since then, she'd never really been the same. She put on a good face, and she hid it well from most people, but it was hard to hide from me and my dad. My heart sank into the pit of my stomach.

"Are you sure she's okay, Dad? I mean I can come back right now, and I can talk to her if you want."

"I don't know if that will help, buddy; I really don't." I heard his voice crack.

"Dad, are you okay?"

His voice was quivering now when he answered, "Buddy, I—I don't know if she's ever coming back."

CHAPTER 4

My brain buzzed in shock, a million signals going off in my head as the rest of my body threatened to go limp. She was gone? What did that mean? Where could she have gone? I mean, for the last five or so years, I'd been the best at helping her. She'd had issues, but we had always gotten through them together. That's what Dad always said, "We'll do it together." But now I wasn't sure, and it was obvious that Dad wasn't sure. His wife had left him. My mother had left me. She was gone—gone.

That word rang loud in my brain as I tried to think of the options. Should I go home? Should I try to find her? If Dad didn't know where she was, how could I? Wait, what about my gift, my extra gift? That could help me, but then again, it had been working in spurts—with uncontrolled on-and-off activity. It wasn't like I could command it by saying, "Abracadabra." It wasn't like I could magically conjure digital coordinates or receive images wired to my head and just fly there on a moment's notice, although that would sure help right about now. I wish it was that easy, but it wasn't.

I tried to control my breathing—one breath in, one breath out. I did that until I counted to fifty, and then I walked off to find my friends—my heart heavy and my stomach churning. Where was Mom?

I didn't say much when I rejoined the others, but I was surprised that Francis had no idea how to fly. He seemed like a smart kid; I guess he had just assumed that we were going to take a plane to Monterey. We'd passed through there on our way down, for no other reason than my dad used to live there when he was a kid, and I wanted to see where he had grown up.

Because Francis was in a wheelchair and nobody else really wanted to carry him—Xander even whispered in my ear that maybe we should leave him behind—it was up to me to fly him. It wasn't hard. I'd flown plenty of people right there next to me who couldn't do what we did, so to take him was really no big deal, but just in case, we waited until it got dark.

You might think that we're crazy to fly in the dark, but it's a lot safer than during the day. A lot less chance of people seeing you or running into something. If you stay at a high enough altitude, especially on the coast, all you have to do is stay a little bit out from the shoreline and you're fine.

Off we went with Francis in tow. Every once in a while I'd glance back at him and his eyes were wide open. He didn't have a helmet, so we had to take things slower than usual. We couldn't fly at the speed of lightning, but we were still going at a pretty good clip. Luckily, he had his thick glasses on; they seemed to help.

We stopped a couple times to eat snacks from the pack that Roy always carried. The easiest snack to bring along was granola bars. I was quiet during most of the stops. Wasn't much to say, especially with my brain whirling, trying to figure out what to do next. Every fiber in my body screamed "leave." I wanted to find my mother. I needed to see if she was okay.

I don't know what I had expected to find when we got to Monterey, but it wasn't this. I'd assumed that Francis and his family had lots of money, which I'm sure they did, but the place we arrived at was pretty modest. Sure, it was on the coast, and it commanded an amazing view of the ocean. But it was far from the impression I had formed in my mind. It was a two-bedroom ranch and pretty humble compared to the Riviera Country Club.

"My grandparents built this place," Francis said as we landed on the front yard and he wheeled himself to the front door. "We used to come here all the time. I used to spend summers here, look out over the ocean and talk to my grandpa who had stories about serving in Vietnam. He was a pretty nice guy and I was sad when he died." It was the first real trace of emotion I had seen from Francis, other than the awe he shown while we were flying.

It served as a reminder that, unlike most of the group, with the exception of Xander, he was all alone in the world. In fact, both Xander and Francis had experienced the loss of their parents. Is that where we were all headed? Dead parents, all of us? We were just kids. How could we deal with that? As I'm telling you what happened, I realize how dark things had become, like there was no hope. My thoughts kept drifting to the worst-case scenario. Death seemed to be all around us.

It was like a creek had trickled into our lives initially, but now a raging river flooded over us with death and destruction. As The Destructors tried to take over, The Keepers were isolated and locked into a realm where we were incapable of helping. The Keepers are historically the saviors of civilization and for centuries helped guide mankind to make the right choices and strive to live with others in harmony. Well, as harmonious as mankind could get. Because let's not kid ourselves, mankind can get pretty screwed up sometimes, and that's what we were seeing now. It seemed right then that humanity was reveling in discord, but only because of the imbalance between The Destructors and The Keepers.

As we entered Francis's house, I thought about what my job entailed, what I was supposed to be doing but how hopeless I felt most days now. Then, an image came into my head, always ghostly, but I knew she was my angel. It was Sybil, the last of The Mystics. She'd come from a long line of them.

They'd helped civilizations for a long time, and Sybil had been ten when she told me that I was to be the last—that I was the one that would carry the torch, and then she'd been gone. Jacee had taken her; but really, Sybil had given herself. She knew what would happen, and she was gone, but I saw her image now. Somehow it comforted me. She had been so strong and hadn't allowed the fear to consume her. I had to be the same. I knew that I needed to be brave for Roy, Jasmine and Lily, Xander and now, Francis.

"There should be some food in the fridge," Francis was saying. "They keep the place stocked for when I come up here. We've got a housekeeping staff that keeps things clean, does the grocery shopping and all that," he said.

He disappeared into the back of the house while the rest of us flopped down on the couches in the living room. Flying could take a lot out of you, especially when you were flying in the middle of the night. You always had to be careful. Hyper-vigilant. So I wasn't surprised when I saw Lily close her eyes and rest her head on Roy's arm. Roy sat straight and stoic as was his nature. Jasmine leaned in the opposite direction resting on a pillow. Xander kicked back, even taking off his shoes and throwing them on the floor.

By the time Francis reentered the main room, I was the only one left awake. I couldn't sleep. I just couldn't make my mind stop. Even with the thought of Sybil bolstering my will, I still found it hard to get peaceful enough to sleep.

"Did you find everything you needed?" Francis asked.

"Yeah, thanks. Did you get what you were looking for?" I asked.

"Not quite. I was hoping that we could make another stop tomorrow morning, if that's okay," Francis said.

"Sure, that shouldn't be a problem. Why don't we get a little bit of sleep and get up early?"

I was trying to be nice. I was trying to be the good guest. I mean, Francis would be learning a lot in the next few weeks, whether he stayed with us or, more likely, stayed at the mansion on Lake Como with my dad and the others.

He was about to turn around and probably head back to his bedroom, but he looked at me. "Could you do me a favor?" he asked with a bit of hesitation in his voice.

"Sure," I said, saying it but not totally meaning it.

He looked uncomfortable, shuffled a little bit in his chair before he asked, "Do you think you could teach me how to fly?"

I smiled, relieved that's all it was. "Of course I will."

I had just fallen asleep when the first rays of dawn beamed through the window. You always think of the sun being something gentle on the horizon, but with my lack of sleep and the troubles I'd had for months now, it always felt like a stabbing light straight from the core of the sun. I opened my eyes just a bit and saw that Roy was already up. The twins were still asleep, Xander too. I smelled bacon and heard sizzling from the vicinity of the kitchen. It was probably Roy, who loved to cook as much as we loved to eat his cooking.

I stifled a groan as I eased myself out of the chair, stretching the kinks out of my neck. When I joined Roy in the kitchen, he was chopping up something on a cutting board. He turned when I entered.

"Hey, did you get any sleep?" he asked. He knew, even though I didn't have to tell him: sleep was not a luxury that I enjoyed enough.

"Yeah. I got a little bit."

"What's on the calendar for today?" he asked. "Are we headed back home, or are we making some more stops?"

Suddenly I remembered that Francis needed something else, that he said he had to tie up some loose ends.

"Francis has something he needs help with. I'm not sure what it is, but he said we could take care of it this morning. Maybe by then I'll have a better picture of what's going on."

He looked at me curiously. It was one of those things. He was always worried about me. He was my protector after all. My bodyguard of sorts and my right-hand man. For some reason, that morning the look annoyed me.

"What?" I asked, a little too sharply.

"I just want to make sure you're okay," he said. "You haven't been yourself lately."

"What do you mean?" I asked.

"I don't know. You're just on edge most of the time."

"Well, wouldn't you be on edge if it was your responsibility to do what we're supposed to be doing?"

"Hey, look," he said. "I'm in this with you. If you need my help, all you need to do is ask. This is all of our responsibility, not just yours."

I heaved a sigh. "I know, and I'm sorry. I'm just tired, frustrated and confused. I just don't know. I thought I was supposed to have all the answers now, and every time I look up, I feel like there are more questions."

"Look," Roy said, turning over the bacon in the frying pan. "Why don't we just take it easy? We could stay here for a couple days. I don't think Francis will mind. You can relax, clear your head and actually get some sleep for a change."

While that sounded tempting, I knew there were things that needed to be done. We had endless responsibilities, saving the world being at the top of the list. Finding, or finding out about my Mom was a close second.

"I don't know. I don't think we can do that," I said. "There's a lot of stuff that needs to be taken care of back in Italy, and, well—" I was about to tell him about Mom, about how she was gone, how she might be gone forever, but then Xander came in.

"Hey, you got any bacon for me?" he asked, pushing past Roy and sticking his fingers into the hot grease. He winced, but he still held a piece of bacon that he blew on as he shuffled it from hand to hand before plopping it in his mouth with great satisfaction.

Roy looked annoyed for a split second but then he smiled. Wasn't that the ultimate compliment to a cook, when you couldn't keep your hands out of a frying pan? "I was just suggesting to Benjamin that maybe we should stay here for a couple days," Roy said.

Xander nodded his agreement. "Yeah. This place isn't so bad. I mean, that couch is a little lumpy, but I can sleep on the floor." If they were expecting a two-day vacation, they were wrong.

Francis dashed those hopes a couple minutes later.

"So what is it you need to do?" I asked, ready to get on the road and to get things done.

"We need to go see somebody."

"Who?" Xander asked, preoccupied with eating his tenth piece of bacon from the hot frying pan.

"Well, we don't really need to see them; we need to—" Francis was looking for the right words. "We need to spy on someone," he said.

Alarm bells rang in my head. What the heck was he talking about?

"Who do you want to spy on?" I asked.

Francis's next words sent sizzling shockwaves through the room. "We need to spy on Jacee Trevane."

CHAPTER 5

My words cut through the air like a bannerman's blade aimed straight at Francis's heart. "What did you say?"

He had looked flip a minute before, but now he glanced around the room, unsure of himself, as if he'd said something stupid. I repeated the question. "What did you say?" The steel in my voice was there for a reason. We were there because of Jacee Trevane—my nemesis, our enemy. He was a person we had been looking for, but couldn't pin down. Now this Francis kid, whoever the heck he was, was saying he wanted to go spy on Jacee. What in the world was going on?

Francis's lips started moving, but no sound came out. And then something strange happened. He reached for his neck. He started turning red. You know, like in Star Wars when Darth Vader used Jedi powers to choke those guys out. Then I realized what was happening.

"Xander, let him go," I said.

"I'm not doing anything," Xander replied with great indignity. I looked at him until I noticed Jasmine in the corner staring intently at Francis, a little smile on her face. I couldn't believe it. I'd never seen Jasmine do anything like this before. That wasn't like her. Sure she could throw out some snarky zingers, but nothing like this. Maybe the pressure was getting to her too.

"Jasmine, let him go." I looked back at Francis, now turning blue. "Let him go, Jasmine. I mean it," I demanded. Just as the kid in the wheelchair started to turn a funky purplish hue, Jasmine released her chokehold. He coughed hard and gulped in a lungful of air.

"Why did you have to do that?" Francis asked, panic registered in his eyes. Between intakes of air, he asked, "Why? What's wrong with you people?"

I ignored his questions. "Whose name did you just say?"

"What—Jacee Trevane? Why shouldn't I say that name? What's wrong with that?" We all stared at him like he was an idiot.

"Seriously? If you had any clue of who Jacee Trevane really is, you would say his name," I said.

Francis actually laughed, "What? Is this like a Harry Potter story? Like he's Voldemort or something so we can't say Jacee Trevane?"

"Maybe we made a mistake coming to find you," I shot back.

"You coming to find me? Maybe I made a mistake coming with you," Francis said. "Maybe I should have done this myself."

Xander laughed, "You have no idea what you're talking about, kid. How the heck would you spy on Jacee Trevane?"

Francis leveled him with a steady glare. "I have a lot more tricks up my sleeve than you think. I might not know how to fly, but I'll bet I can take down Jacee Trevane."

It was Lily who spoke up next, "What do you have against him?"

This time Francis's eyes softened. I thought I even saw a light glaze in his eye, like he was going to cry, but he didn't. Instead he said, "Jacee Trevane killed my parents."

CHAPTER 6

After a full minute of silence, Xander said, "Jeez…." I was at a loss for words. I mean, shouldn't Francis have said something when we first picked him up? Why had he kept it to himself? Then it reminded me of when Xander had been working for Jacee, when he let Trevane track us. He'd even carried the tracking beacon himself, deep into the Amazon forest. Was this the same thing? Was Francis playing us?

"How do you know he killed your parents?" Roy asked, his voice level and calm.

"I just know, okay?" Francis said. "I just know. I just—what does it matter, anyway? None of you guys are saying he didn't. Are you telling me he didn't?" No one answered.

Lily asked, "How do you know that Jacee killed your parents?"

"Well, they died in Los Angeles, didn't they? In the big thing that everybody's calling national disasters or whatever? I mean, Jacee's behind that, right?"

"How do we know that you aren't trying to trick us?" Jasmine asked. She stepped closer, and Francis actually moved his wheelchair back. The thought of getting choked out by a girl with telekinetic powers was obviously too much for him. All the smugness had left him. I saw one tear followed by another streak his face.

"What would you do if he killed your parents, huh?" He was sniffling now, trying to hold back the tears, but it was no use. They were coming. I knew that feeling. "None of you have disputed the fact that he did kill my parents. Is it true? Is he behind everything? Is he the one? Am I right?" Again a pause—the rest of us knowing the truth—but we never shared those secrets with the outside world. Even if Francis was one of us, he hadn't earned our trust yet.

"What if we told you it was true?" I asked, the words coming out slowly so he wouldn't miss a one. "What would you do then? Would you seek revenge? Would you try to kill him?"

We needed to know where this kid stood. If he was going to be one of us, we had to know, one way or the other. But how would we even know if he was telling the truth? I mean, I didn't blame Jasmine for choking him, but we didn't really know what his past was like. We didn't know what he'd been through. Even though I wished I did, I didn't have a litmus test in my brain that told me whether this kid was good or bad. My powers didn't work that way, unfortunately.

"I don't know what I'd do, okay?" Francis sniffed. "I just—I don't know. Maybe I'll just talk to him or maybe I'll just say some bad words or something. I don't know. I mean—look at me. I've been in a wheelchair for as long as I can remember. Do you think I have the power to do what you're saying? Do you think I can really get revenge on Jacee Trevane? I don't know if I can. Maybe I will, with your help, but what I really want to do is stop everything that's happening. If he's behind it, he killed my parents and all those others out there. How can we let him keep doing what he's doing, then show up on TV and act like he's a hero? Seriously? How long is he going to get away with that?"

It might have sounded like a series of honest questions, something straight from the heart, but to me, it was more like an accusation that we had fallen asleep on the job. I really felt like I was the one who was supposed to stop him; that we, The Keepers, were supposed to stop him, but up to that point no chance had materialized. After Jacee Trevane's debut on TV, when it first started, he kept making appearances, but as soon as we got there, he'd disappear. He was good at hiding. He had his underground network, and all we could do was keep looking through our proverbial haystack.

Roy put a huge hand on my shoulder, as if he sensed my pain, as if he sensed the guilt that I carried every day. It was a burden that he tried to take from me, but he couldn't, and he knew that. I took a quick breath, and I exhaled, trying to get rid of my frustration. It wasn't Francis's fault. I mean, his parents were dead after all, and Jacee was behind it. For all we knew, he was behind everything. Even though we didn't have the evidence, everything pointed toward Trevane.

"Okay. Let's assume he did do it," I said. "What then? How can you help us?"

"We can't trust him," Jasmine hissed, the anger thrown at me like a dart. I looked at her, totally confused by what she was saying. She was usually so quiet. Well, of the two, Lily was probably the quieter, but Jasmine never got angry. Neither of them did. They always held in their emotions. They never liked to show weakness, and I respected that, so to see her now throwing barbs at me and Francis, caught me off guard. I put up a hand.

"Let him talk, Jasmine, please. I want to hear what he has to say." Jasmine didn't nod and she kept a steely gaze on Francis.

Finally, Francis answered, "I've got resources, too. I can help in my own way, if that's what you guys need. I'm happy to do it."

"Are you sure you know what you're offering?" I asked. "There's a lot of danger involved. We've almost been killed too many times to count. Are you sure you're ready for that, to put your life on the line? Looks like you could live a pretty good life up here. You've got the money; you probably have the power. You can enjoy life. Why join us? Why try to save the world from Jacee Trevane, other than revenge?"

It took Francis a few moments to gather his thoughts and to give us the answer.

"I've never been part of something, okay? Even my parents thought I was a freak kid in a wheelchair. They didn't like to take me out in public. Sure, they loved me in their own way, but I was just a sideshow for them—someone they could throw money at in an effort to keep me entertained. They gave me my video games, let me sit by the pool while the other kids swam, looking at me and whispering behind my back. How do you think that made me feel? I can tell you: worthless. Well, now I feel like I can do something. I feel like I can use these gifts, powers, or whatever you call them for good to help the world. If that's what you guys are doing, then I want to help. I have a way I can, but if you don't want me with you, then I'll go it alone. I'll figure it out. I may not be as powerful as you guys, but I can figure it out. I always have."

The tension in the room eased with Francis's explanation. I knew the others were waiting for me to make the decision.

After all I was their appointed leader, the guy they voted to spearhead the effort to save humanity. I was the guy who had to make the decision. I could either send him to Italy, or he could come with us. There was even the option of leaving him behind. I had no idea how he could help, but as I looked at him, his eyes pleading, I realized that he was me. He was all of us. We'd all been through it. We were all freaks and damaged in our own way. He was just the latest crop. What to do? Suddenly there was only one answer.

"Okay, Francis," I said. "Tell us what you have in mind."

A short time later, we touched down outside the well-manicured estate that Francis said was owned by the Trevane Corporation. Francis had told us his plan before we left the house, and while it sounded kind of crazy and like it might not work, I always knew we could fly out of there if we had to. Besides, I wasn't the only one curious about what Francis could do.

On the short ride over, we opted to take a cab instead of flying. You know, with it being the middle of the morning and all, better safe than sorry. We did hop a quick flight over when we realized that we'd have to climb down a ravine if we were going to be able to come in unseen.

When I asked Francis how he knew so much about the area, he explained that he had "resources." I didn't really know what that meant. I took him at his word. He had been pretty upfront about everything with us so far. Why not trust him further? We could always bolt if we needed to.

"I'm actually surprised that he doesn't have sensors and crazy cameras all over his property," Francis was thinking out loud. "He's got some heavily armed security patrols with dogs. Those shouldn't be a problem. My people said they don't patrol as much in the morning. They are more active patrolling during the afternoon, and especially at night. Our timing is kind of perfect right now."

He was right. When we got to a point with a good vantage of the entire property (which was huge, by the way), we could see that there were sets of guards over by the house huddled together, chatting, their dogs lying nearby. The dogs couldn't smell us from that distance. Heck, we probably smelled like deer anyway. I can't remember the last time we'd showered.

"So what now?" I asked.

Francis hadn't been upfront. He hadn't told us everything. He said he had a plan, but who knew what it involved? I wasn't expecting what came out of his mouth next.

"I thought I'd use myself as bait," he said. "I can go in and talk to them and tell them to come outside. Then you guys could grab them or whatever you planned on doing. Does that work?"

That was the last thing I thought he'd say.

"I don't get it. I thought you said you wanted to spy on them," I said. "Now you want to give yourself up? What if something happens?"

Francis gave me a wry grin. "Are you saying you're going to let something happen or is this just a worst-case scenario type of thing?"

That actually made me smile. I was starting to like the kid. Sure, he still kind of acted like he owned the world.

Something about his confidence made me feel more confident, something I should've been feeling on my own.

"Okay. If you think that'll work, I think we can cover you. That is, unless The Destructors are all over the place."

"Who are The Destructors?" Francis asked.

Xander laughed, "You've got a lot to learn, kid. The Destructors are the bad guys. Those are the guys that Jacee leads. We don't want any piece of them right now. Sure, we could take a bunch. But who knows how many are in there?"

Francis thought about that for a second and then said, "Maybe you're right. Maybe there's a better way to get—" He paused. "Why didn't I think of it before? Okay, give me a minute. Let me make a phone call. I'll see if I can get this thing done."

After a hushed conversation on his phone and commands that sounded more like they were coming from a CEO than a kid, Francis hung up. "Okay. It's all set. He should be getting the call in a minute. Say in about ten minutes, he'll be outside. Does that work? Is that enough time?"

"Hold on a minute. Will what work? Who is he?" I asked. "What are we supposed to be doing?"

"We're going to nab Jacee, right?" Francis said. "You guys can do that. Can't you like use your powers and make him come with you by lifting him off the ground and then hold him down or something like that?"

I looked at Roy and the others. Roy shrugged. "I guess it could work," Roy said. "Again, The Destructors—what if he comes out with a bunch of them?"

"Look, I said I'd take care of it," Francis said. "Jacee will come out by himself. Everybody else will stay in the house. It's part of what I requested."

He said it in a way that—I don't know—it made me feel like he was used to orchestrating things. Sure enough, in just under ten minutes, Jacee Trevane, the man himself—the guy I hadn't seen in five years in person—strolled out the back door and walked around the pool.

He had a phone in his hand. I could see that now. We had brought binoculars so we could take a look. He was pacing and waiting. I don't know for what. I guess it was part of Francis's plan. Then, a moment later, I heard a buzzing overhead and looked up.

"Right on time," Francis said, grinning, looking up toward a speck in the sky.

One of those helicopter drones came into view and made a beeline for the backyard. Jacee was looking up at it, holding his phone to his ear like he was receiving instructions. I saw his mouth moving. I had no idea who he was talking to or why he was letting the helicopter drone continue toward him. It came in closer, slowing as it descended. Then, it was right overhead.

I saw Jacee put up his hand like he was going to grab something. Then, to his surprise, and to ours, something fell out and went *poof*. There was no real audible sound, except maybe a little bit of a cracking sound. It was more like a smoke grenade or something. All I know is as soon as it happened, the entire area surrounding Jacee was enveloped in smoke—almost black smoke.

I didn't hesitate. I reached out using my gift. I grabbed where I remembered Jacee was, whisking him carefully over the fence, through the ravine, and back toward us. I smelled the smoke now as I brought him down, careful to contain his body in what I would simply describe as a capsule of my gift. Kind of like a jail made out of air that nobody can get out of.

The last thing I wanted was for Jacee to start using his powers on us. We had to keep him contained. Everybody was at the ready, staring at the swirling smoke. Then I let it go. The smoke dissipated as the ocean air took it away on its breeze. Jacee stood staring at me. His eyes were wide but they held no anger.

"Wait a minute," I said to myself. Something wasn't right; something wasn't right at all. Those eyes—they weren't the same eyes that I remembered. They weren't Jacee's eyes.

"Who are you?" I asked with panic beginning to rise in my throat, tasting like bile. "Who are you?" I emphasized each word and sounded quite scared, even to my ears.

The rest of my friends looked at me, completely confused, like I was going nuts or something.

My impatience was like a piece of dynamite that had just been ignited. "I said who are you?" I asked again, this time with more force. I moved forward, like I was going to grab him by the front of his shirt. Actually, I was pinning him with my mind, his arms completely pressed against his flanks. His feet were glued to the ground. He couldn't move except for his mouth—I made sure of that.

When his voice came out, it sounded completely different than I remembered, completely different than the voice we'd heard on TV so many times. The voice wasn't confident and most definitely not the cocky one I remembered from Jacee. This was not the world leader who'd taken the helm and was supposedly saving humanity, so to speak.

No, this was someone else entirely. Then he said, "It's not my fault; it's not my fault. He made me do it."

Suddenly, out of the corner of my eye, I saw it. Movement from the back of Jacee's compound. Black figures all in a line, streaming from the house like ants. Then they were in the air shooting straight at us, like arrows darting across the expanse.

Francis looked at me in complete horror, like his plan had gone completely sideways.

"We have to go," I said with a calm I didn't quite feel.

The rest of the team was already thinking in that direction. I focused on Francis instead of the man that was supposed to be Jacee. And with one final look back, we were gone.

CHAPTER 7

They flew after us like a swarm of locusts. There was something different this time. It had been close to a year since we'd been chased, but we had our routine down. However, something was definitely different. Then I realized there were more of them than before and they had become more organized. We had practiced getaways until we could practically do them in our sleep. We skimmed the earth, barely three feet above the surface. A tree whipped me on the leg as we zoomed past. Luckily, I had been smart enough to put my helmet on, but Francis wasn't so lucky. He held his hands over his eyes, both to hold his glasses down and to protect himself from the whipping wind. I could only imagine what he was thinking, even though I was ticked off that he'd put us in this position.

We were in an inverted V formation, with me leading and Roy not far behind. I knew what the others were doing; they were focusing on objects on the ground. Tossing them back like chaff from a jet that was trying to get away from its pursuer or trying to dodge a missile. We weren't very different from that. I chanced a look back and saw that there were fewer chasers now. Some of our pursuers had been knocked out of the sky or maybe had just crashed, but there were still plenty left to take us down. Left and right we swerved, our formation inching farther and farther apart, for safety's sake. We'd be of no use if we all got taken out by something just because we were huddled together. That would be stupid.

We were just cresting a tall hill that overlooked the countryside beyond. The plan I had just created was to shoot up for the clouds since they were pretty low that day. It was easy to lose followers up in the clouds. I started to signal to my friends what my plan was. We had perfected basic hand signals ages ago.

Then it hit me like a searing dagger to the skull, right between my eyes. I felt blazing pain. "NO," the voice screamed in my head. I knew it was the old voice, the one that had been calling for help. Now it distracted me from what I was supposed to be doing. When I next opened my eyes, I realized that Francis was falling to the ground, his face now a mask of terror as he tumbled and tumbled. Luckily, it happened when we were flying at a higher altitude, and not three feet off the ground, or else he might already be dead.

I quickly regained my senses, snatched him up, and he was next to me in the blink of an eye. Then I signaled to my friends, and we shot skyward toward the clouds—toward safety—away from The Destructors. For good measure, I ripped out a few pine trees, using my powers, and tossed them back into the ranks of The Destructors. I didn't look to see if I'd hit anything; that wasn't really the purpose. I was just hoping to gain an extra second or two to help us get away.

By the time we hit the lip of the cloud, we were all together again. Hands held again, just like we'd practiced, time and time again. I led the way at half the speed we had been going, counting down the seconds. Thirty, twenty-nine, twenty-eight, twenty-seven, twenty-six—. When I reached zero, I slowed down to a complete stop. We all just waited, hovering high in the air, like hummingbirds. Surrounded by pure quiet, it was an eerie feeling. We all looked at each other, waiting.

During a time like this, it was important to be patient. Like a high-stakes game of hide-and-seek, the first person to move usually lost. I had not planned to lose. My head still ached from the scream moments before, but at least now I could focus. Part of my mind tackled the task at hand; another part thought about where the scream had originated. It had been so urgent, so pained and sounded like a warning. It had been different, like someone screaming before seeing a criminal shoot a loved one. The pain—I could feel it—I could taste it. It tasted like acidic blood, the taste of iron in my mouth.

"What do we do now?" Francis whispered. I put a finger to my lips, demanding silence. He nodded his acceptance to my order, his eyes wide, still teary from the flight. Then I nodded to the others, and we took off slowly. Painfully slow, careful to stay within the billowy cloud cover. What we needed now was time. Time to ask questions of Francis.

"What in the world was that all about?"

"How was I supposed to know that wasn't him?" Francis asked.

We'd been grilling him for a good fifteen minutes. I was a pretty good judge of character, and it was plainly obvious that he wasn't lying. He'd been as shocked as we were. On any other day his plan might have worked. The whole drone smoke bomb thing was actually a pretty good idea when you thought about it. When things go sideways, it's hard not to scrutinize the person who came up with the plan.

Once again it was Jasmine who was taking the lead, whipping out questions like she was slapping Francis in the face. Every once in a while Xander would get a "Yeah" in, or an "I told you we shouldn't have trusted him."

The conversation became more heated. More questions. More back and forth. Francis was getting defensive and louder now, and I could see why. I was about to cut in to tell everyone to be quiet or else we'd be found. But then my vision went blank, like somehow the clouds we were hovering in solidified, leaving me blind and mute. The scream came again, but this time stabbing even deeper in my head—if that were even possible.

"No! No!" One final scream in my head and my vision cleared, but it wasn't what I'd just been looking at. My friends weren't there. It was a coastal city—one that looked like—My gosh, it was Monterey. I knew what I had to do.

I blinked twice as I came out of the trance. My friends were there again, looking at me with concern, especially Roy. I turned to him.

"You have to take Francis to safety. I need to go see something."

"What is it, Benjamin?" Roy asked.

"It's not safe here," I said. "Take everybody south. I'll call you when I know."

"Know what?" Xander asked.

"He's had a vision," Lily answered for me. "Haven't you, Benjamin?"

I looked into those inquisitive eyes of hers. I nodded.

"It's not safe," I repeated. "You guys have to go. I promise I'll meet you there."

Roy looked unsure, like he wanted to come with me. He never wanted me to go off alone. It was his duty, as he saw it, to keep me safe; but I was perfectly able to protect myself, and he knew that.

"Just go. Take them," I urged.

Without another word, I was off flying as quick as I could go, through the clouds, as hard as my body could take it. The air hammered my body with pain, but I ignored it, pushing on toward the vision that I had seen.

I flew over the golf courses. Pebble Beach, Spyglass and the others that my dad had played at over the years. He'd told me about them and I'd visited them on our way through.

It was an upward ascent, through Carmel and over to Monterey. I was careful to keep most of my body concealed in the clouds, my head peeking out. Everything looked as it should. People were driving, walking down the streets, pushing baby strollers, but the fear pushed me onward. I knew what was going to happen. I had seen it, like I'd been looking through someone else's eyes.

Then I was there in the coastal city that ramped up into the hills. I had arrived in Monterey, where the otters played in the kelp beds on the coast and the Monarch butterflies flocked to the hills every year. I couldn't go any further without being seen, because the clouds disappeared just past the city. I wanted to see and I wanted to stop, with all my heart, whatever was coming. Whatever it was that I had been alerted about.

Suddenly, I heard the sound, a deep grumbling, like Earth was waking up from a long slumber, and then the rumbling started. The surface of the Earth began tumbling and vibrating. I saw a building start to shake, even wobble, but I knew the worst was yet to come. Then the destruction happened, in one awful moment, like a gigantic sinkhole.

The coastal land was swallowed along with the hills for miles and miles. It happened fast. There wasn't enough time for the screams of everyone just taken to their deaths to be heard or even sounded. I watched in horror as yet another city was destroyed, wiped off the face of the Earth, reclaimed by the inside of the world. The deep sadness almost overwhelmed me. It threatened to plunge me to the earth, dashing me on the rocks below, and then I realized it wasn't my sadness. Although I was profoundly shocked by what I'd just seen, the deep sadness belonged to the eyes I had seen the initial vision through. That person and I were linked. I felt the sadness keenly, like it was my own, like I possessed the other's body and it possessed mine.

In that moment I knew that whoever was behind that vision, whoever was behind those cries for help, was the one who had caused the devastation. I finally had a glimpse into Jacee Trevane's plan. I now knew what his weapon was. It was a person. A person of great power. A person who was shackled and being used. With a final whisper in my head, like a loved one bidding a mournful good-bye, it told me its name—The Ancient.

CHAPTER 8

You might think that the idea of a single person creating such havoc would make me even more scared; that I would run away, find my friends and look for the darkest place we could find to hide. But it had the exact opposite effect on me. It actually gave me hope.

If there was only one person behind it, we could deal with it. We could find that person, and if he or she was in trouble—being controlled—maybe we could help that person and save him.

I tried to call back, tried to use my mind to tell that person I understood—that I knew what he were going through—that we were there to help. But there was nothing. I didn't know if I was doing it wrong, because I'd never done it before. I'd never before tried to answer the voice I heard.

Prior to this new development, I had visions. I saw pictures or images, like silent movies I watched in my head. Never voices. No one talking to me. This was something new. Was this how The Mystics of old used to communicate with each other? Maybe they did when they traveled Earth, helping civilizations. How else would they communicate? In Ancient Rome, they didn't have cell phones, and if someone they needed was in China, how would they coordinate any kind of effort? Was it possible that this person, The Ancient, was also a mystic? Could Sybil could have lied to me? What if she just hadn't known? I quickly dismissed that idea. That's not the vibe I'd gotten from the one-way conversation I'd just had.

I knew The Ancient was a Destructor. He could be The Destructor, the most powerful gifted person ever to step foot on Earth. But if it was possible for him to talk to me, without the use of technology, would that help us in the future or would it just be another pain for me? Was this even something I wanted to share with my friends? I could imagine Jasmine grilling me about it and Xander wanting to be in my head just because he was like that. He was my brother, but that never stopped him from giving me a hard time.

I would have to be selective with what I told them. I took the time as I flew over where the Monterey Bay Aquarium used to be, where men and women had just been golfing on the greens, and I tried to figure out what I would tell my friends. What was our new course of action? They all looked to me. Really, the plan was obvious. We had to find Jacee again because I had a feeling that where he was, The Ancient was as well. But that meant there would also be a lot of Destructors. If a few minutes before had been any indication of what they were doing now, Jacee had definitely swelled his ranks. More people recruited to protect him and his new weapon.

I flew on with the hope that maybe Francis could locate Jacee again. He'd done it once, but as soon as I rejoined them and asked Francis how he'd done it before, he quickly dismissed my idea. "The only reason I got that close before," he explained, "was because he thought I was on his side. Now that he knows I'm with you guys, there's no way we'll be able to find him."

"But, how'd you find him before?" Xander asked. "I mean you were spot on. You knew that whole place."

Francis nodded. "It took me weeks to discover that place, and then it took even more time to scope it all out in order to set up a plan. Ten dollars says that after the stunt we pulled today, he'll have that compound's security even tighter and better fortified."

But I wasn't convinced or taking the bet. There had to be another way.

It was no use staying in California; there wasn't anything left for us to do. The whole recruiting trip had just been an excuse to kill time. Anybody could do that. The good part about my visions and my ability to find the newly gifted was that I could tell exactly where those people were and learn their names. Once I had that information, I could pass on those details; somebody else could go get them. Now it was urgent to return to our home in Italy. Something told me that Italy was where it all originated—the genesis, if you will. So much of our history had been linked to that country.

While you'd probably think we'd just hop in the air and fly to Italy, it's not quite that easy. Well, I'm sure it could be done and I'm sure plenty of people had done it or at least tried it, but that's a long flight. Unless you're wearing some kind of special trans-atlantic suit or in some kind of crazy, futuristic capsule, your body can't go as fast as an airplane. I don't care what Xander says. But we did have a private account with a jet company that could fly us anywhere we wanted. After a quick call to our Lake Como Travel Department, as Jasmine had named it, we were on our way to San Jose to catch a flight back home. Once we were airborne and the stewardess had gotten our orders for drinks and food, we retreated to the back of the cabin.

The six of us were the only ones flying that day. That was how it usually was. You might think that the pilots and the crew would think that a bunch of teenagers traveling alone would be weird, but it's funny what money can do. Besides, they were paid to be discreet. It's what they did. It's what they were signed up for. As we gathered in the back of the plane, they left us alone.

"Are you sure this is the best idea?" Roy asked as he took a seat next to me. "I mean, we had Jacee's location. Maybe we should have stayed."

I raised my hand to silence his coming thoughts. "No, Roy. We've got to go home. You need to trust me on this, okay?"

I'd seen it—I still saw it—I heard it. I'd already told them all about my vision about the one behind it, The Ancient. While Francis was the only one who seemed skeptical, the others believed me. We'd been through a lot. They knew what I was capable of, what I'd seen before. I kept seeing a new hope that things might be changing, that our luck had just changed for the better.

"Man, I bet The Ancient is some wrinkled dude that looks like a mummy," Xander was saying, laughing. "You'd think he was like an ancient Egyptian or maybe he was King Tut's buddy? Come on, Benjamin. Tell us what he looks like."

I shrugged my shoulders. "I have no idea what the guy looks like. I just saw what he saw, and I heard his voice."

"Tell us again what it sounded like," Lily said. She'd been analyzing everything I'd told her. She was good at processing things, kind of like our own human calculator or personal computer.

I closed my eyes. I tried to remember exactly what The Ancient had sounded like. "He was quiet the first couple times," I said, remembering when The Ancient had called for help. "Almost like he had just woken up or maybe as if he had been drugged or something."

Lily nodded, her eyes still pinched. "Maybe that's how Jacee does it," she said. "Maybe that's how they keep him under control—keep him drugged. But how could someone that powerful not get away?"

I shook my head. We still had too many questions and not enough answers.

"Maybe he'll call you again," Roy said, "hopefully."

"Yeah," Xander agreed, putting a finger in the air. "Kind of like ET phone home." That cut the tension and we all chuckled. Well, all except Francis. He'd been quiet ever since take-off.

"Hey, are you okay?" I asked him.

He looked up. "What? Uh, yeah. I was just thinking. You know, again, I'm really sorry about what happened. I just—"

"It's not your fault," I said. "You had no way of knowing, and in fact, I have a feeling it had more to do with me than it did you."

Francis's eyes widened. "You? Why?"

"Because he hates me," I said. "Jacee Trevane tried to recruit me, just like he tried to recruit you and all the others."

"Yeah, but Benjamin, good ole Benjamin. He took care of Jacee," Xander said, patting me on the back. "Good ole Jacee is scared of our Benjamin."

Francis looked at everyone's face for confirmation. He got nods in return. "But I was the one who took you to his place. I was the one spying and playing double agent," he said, still trying to take the blame.

I shook my head. "Look, if there's anything we've learned, it's that taking any of this personally is no good. Jacee Trevane is the one to blame. The ones who went with him are to blame. Not us. Our only real chance of beating him is to do our best to keep this from happening again. Trust me. It's best to look at the good side and not dwell on the bad."

He still didn't look convinced, but then he cocked his head and grinned. A little grin, but still a grin. "You mean like the glass that's half full," he said.

I returned his smile. "Yeah, something like that."

CHAPTER 9

The flight over the Atlantic was uneventful and, for the first time in who knows how long, I slept. I didn't just nap like I usually did on those transatlantic flights, but I slept and I slept hard.

When the pilot announced that we were going to land in fifteen minutes, I woke but couldn't remember what I had dreamed about. In fact, it felt like I hadn't had any dreams at all. It had been like a quiet sleep in some deep, dark, safe cave, like my body and mind were being prepared for something, and prepared they were. My mind felt clean and crisp like it had just been washed and buffed. It's funny what clarity can do for you, even when you know you're probably flying right into the eye of the storm.

From Rome it was a helicopter hop over to Lake Como, and as we descended over the blue water I caught a glimpse of my home—of our home. For five years it had been the only place we felt safe. Our lair, so to speak, where we would be safe and could just relax. The mansion was nestled into the base of what I can only describe as a mini-mountain.

While the mansion itself looked impressive from the outside and especially from the air, it was what was beneath it, and beneath the mountain, that was truly impressive. I knew that since we'd been gone, there had been more of our kind descending on Lake Como, both for safekeeping and for training. The mansion—my family's ancestral home—was a perfect place for both. To our knowledge, none of The Destructors aligned with Jacee knew our location, and the underground tunnels and caverns that we'd built were perfect for training.

As we descended to the manicured lawn of the mansion, I scanned the area for my father, half expecting to see Mom too, but no one was there to greet us. Just another day at the mansion on Lake Como. That was actually fine with me. I needed to stay busy, and if I had seen my dad at that moment, I might have asked about my mom, and a discussion about her whereabouts wasn't going to help my clarity any. I needed to stay focused and believed that if I kept that laser sight on my next target, everything would be well. That Mom would be safe too.

We scattered when we entered the front of the house. Roy suggested that he take Francis to what we called our Welcome Center, the place where the gifted who just arrived were checked in, given a room and told what to expect. I honestly didn't know if Francis had a part to play in the upcoming drama. Time would tell and, after his initial screening with the mansion staff, we'd know what Francis's capabilities truly were.

I found Dad in the library in his usual spot. He'd rather be surrounded by books than in some stuffy office. He said it inspired him, being surrounded by so many figures of literature and of history. He even started writing his own book a year ago, something about the fall of Rome. He was keeping it pretty quiet, and I never pressed, but I think it had something to do with explaining to the world that what history had taught us wasn't exactly the truth.

Now, I'm not sure if you remember, but we've discussed before that the fall of Rome had more to do with my people, with the gifted, than anything else. It had been the last real war between The Destructors and The Keepers, so Dad definitely had to be careful about what he wrote, since we'd already gotten in trouble for documenting our own history.

Sybil had taught me that, too. We didn't need to write our history down. We lived our history. As long as we were together, the Keepers would be one, and we would survive. Dad didn't notice when I walked in. There were enough people coming in and out that looking up every time someone entered the door was a waste of time. I nodded to a couple of familiar faces, and I then walked up behind my dad.

"How's the book coming?" I asked. He turned quickly, and when he did, I had to bite my tongue not to gasp. My dad's eyes were bloodshot. Dark bags hung under them. His skin was pale, far from the tan complexion I was used to. My dad was one of those guys that everybody wanted to be. He was good looking and athletic, but now he looked twenty years older.

I forced the same contrived smile onto my face that he did, and I gratefully accepted his hug. "Hey bud, I didn't know you were coming home today," he said. Another clue that something wasn't right.

I'd told my dad when I was coming home. He should've had my itinerary. Someone normally would have told him, too. Reminded him that his son was coming home.

"I didn't want to bother you," I lied, trying to play along. "I figured you had enough on your hands."

He held me at arm's length, looking me up and down. I saw a tear there, but he blinked it away. "You look good, bud. How are things?"

I'd already told him about Francis, and of course he knew about what had happened in Monterey. I was about to tell him about the flight over, but then his eyes glazed over, like he'd suddenly lost all interest.

"Dad, are you okay?" I asked, truly concerned now. I had never seen my father this distracted and forlorn. Sure, there have been times when I've been concerned about him, when he'd been too worried about Mom and hadn't taken care of himself, but this felt different. I've never seen my father afraid. Now he looked truly afraid.

"Yeah, I'm fine," he answered, waving a hand like it didn't matter. "Got a lot on my plate. You know, that, and—well, I've just got a lot on my plate." I wanted to look him in the eye and tell him that everything was going to be okay, but was it really? I had no idea where Mom was, and it looked like he didn't either, but I wasn't done. I needed him in that moment. I needed him to listen to me. Maybe I could help him snap out of his funk, let him know that there was hope on the horizon.

"I've got a lead on who's behind all this," I said. That got his attention.

"Did you see something? Do you know what's been going on?"

It had originally been my dad who'd come up with the idea of a lot of The Destructors getting together to do what had been done to the major cities around the world, so I figured that telling him about The Ancient might get him thinking down another avenue, away from Mom, away from the grief.

"There's one person behind it all, Dad. I saw it. I saw it through his eyes," I proclaimed, but Dad didn't look surprised. In fact, there was something else there. Something that made me realize that I'd read it all wrong.

"What do you know, Benjamin? What did you see?" he asked, his voice shaking.

I told him about the cries for help and about the call right before Monterey was destroyed. I was about to tell him about The Ancient—that there was a single man behind it all—but he interrupted me. His face was plaster gray and I saw a sheen of sweat followed by tears. His mouth opened but no words came out for a moment.

"So you know," he croaked. "Oh God, you know."

My stomach twisted and I asked, "What are you saying, Dad? What's wrong?"

He wasn't listening now, just shaking his head, the tears flowing. I wanted to tell him that it was okay, that it was The Ancient behind it, and that maybe we could find him and bring him back into our community. As I was about to tell him, Dad blurted, "Benjamin, it's your mother who's behind it all."

CHAPTER 10

What was my dad talking about? There was no way that Mom could be behind it, no way. "Dad, that's impossible. I saw him; they call him The Ancient. That's who was behind all this. That's who Jacee's been controlling to do what they've done."

Dad was still shaking his head. "No. You're wrong, Benjamin. I should've told you before, but I really thought she would get better. When I told you she had left that wasn't everything. I really think," he gulped audibly. "I really think she's going to hurt herself. She's going to do something. She feels bad. She said it's all her fault—that she did it—that she was the one behind it."

A stab of despair punctured my chest. "Dad, I'm telling you there is no way Mom could be the one. There is no way."

"You're wrong, Benjamin," he said, frantic now. "We've been so wrong, even the doctor—the one in Switzerland. It was all a lie, all of it." Dad was battling now. I had to grab him by the shoulders to steady him.

"Dad, tell me everything. Tell me what you know," Dad looked around suddenly like he just realized that we were in public and that people could hear him.

"Come on," he said. "Let's go to my room. I guess I'll tell you there." He half dragged me behind him. I knew, if we didn't get there in time, the information would never come out of his mouth.

When we got through the massive doors leading into the master bedroom, he slammed the huge portal shut and slumped into a chair. I felt like the parent now, like I was the one taking care of him. In a soothing tone I asked, "How did it all start, Dad? Just tell me. All of it...from the beginning." He wiped his face slowly, and then looked at me, refocused and nodded.

"You remember when your mother was taken?"

I nodded, of course I remembered. I mean, I didn't remember the actual act. I had just seen the consequences. Mom was in hysterics, shaking and yelling at me from within the bedroom closet. Jacee and his cronies had done something to my mom; I didn't know what. She'd never actually told me. I don't even know if she ever told Dad, but they had tortured her in some way. I think they scrambled her brain or something. There had been spells of peace since then, but the pain always returned.

"I didn't know how bad it had gotten, until just before she left," my dad said. "She never told me the whole thing. She said the doctor in Switzerland had come very highly recommended and that those first few sessions had helped. It was supposed to be some kind of counseling, like the stuff war vets get. She couldn't remember anything about what had happened. She just knew about the pain that had been left. So part of the doctor's job was to get to those memories, find the answers, and get to the root of the problem. They never got to the root of the problem before they ended the work.

"She said the doctor had told her that more extreme measures would be needed, that mere counseling wouldn't work, so he did other things. Now remember—your mother was desperate. She wanted help; she really thought this doctor was helping. They tried hypnosis, and that seemed to help a bit. Some memories were jogged, but she also admitted to me that there were parts of each session that she could not remember. Maybe the doctor had put her under only to implant something else. Then he moved onto more invasive things: shock therapy and injections." A sob escaped my dad's mouth. "Oh God, Benjamin. I can't imagine what you must think. I should've been there to protect her. I should've known."

While I felt the horror of the words, I somehow moved past it, trying to put the two together, The Ancient and my mother. I knew without a doubt that The Ancient was a completely different person. He was the one behind it, not my mother. I had to get to the bottom of that first. That was something I could fix.

"Dad, what did Mom say about the attacks? Why did she say that *she* did it?"

Dad stared at me, like uttering the words would be too awful for me to comprehend. Then he spoke, "She described each one, Benjamin. Every one, down to the most minute of details. She said she had no recollection of being there, but that she'd seen it all. That she just blanked—just like in the sessions with the doctor."

I thought about my visions, about the telepathic link that I'd had with The Ancient. Maybe the same thing had happened with my mom—that could explain it. Maybe I wasn't the only one that could do what we'd done. That left me with a question, one that came out of my mouth slowly so my dad could fully hear me.

"Are you sure that's what she said, Dad? Are you sure that's how she explained it?"

Dad nodded, "She was there, Benjamin. She was there, and I know it."

"But you said she saw it, Dad. Maybe it was just like my thing, where she has visions."

Dad shook his head violently, "No. I didn't explain it right. That's not what I meant. Yes, she saw it, but it was when she came to. Ah jeez, Benjamin. I don't know what you must think right now."

"Dad, tell me," I said forcefully.

"When she came to, she was there. She was standing outside the area of destruction. She was there, Benjamin."

My resolve wavered. Maybe it wasn't just a vision; maybe she had done it. I slapped the thought away. There's no way my mother could do that. Then snapshots of Monterey flickered in my head.

"Dad, what about Monterey? There's no way she could have been there. That would've been way too much of a coincidence. I was there. There's no way I could've missed her."

This time, his head shake was slow and sad. He looked at me. Completely distraught, "That's what I've been trying to tell you," he said. "She was there; I know she was there."

"How? Did you talk to her? Did she call you?" I don't know if it pained me more that Mom had been there and could've been behind the destruction of the city or that she'd known that I was in Monterey and hadn't called me.

"She told me she was going there," Dad said.

"But why? Why would she go there?"

When he looked up at me this time, his eyes blazed with the first hint of anger I'd seen in a while. The words came out like the hiss of a python, “She went to Monterey to confront that bastard—Jacee Trevane.”

CHAPTER 11

I don't remember walking back to my room or getting in bed. I must have brushed my teeth at some point, because in the middle of the night, I woke up with the faint minty taste of my toothpaste on my tongue. I did something I'd never done before; I dove too deep, using my dreams as a tool, sifting through memories one at a time. I thought that I'd be freaking out at this point, that what my dad had told me would have sent me over the edge, but it hadn't. It did confuse me for sure, but I didn't—couldn't—believe that my mom was behind it.

Deeper and deeper I went. Some of the memories were thick like mud, like quicksand sucking me in, so I would quickly jump out. Other memories were light and airy, filled with good memories of me, my friends and my parents. Like a riot of leaves on a soft breeze, we were like pebbles skipping on water. Occasionally, I would wake and sometimes I would see a face looking at me. Mainly it was Roy looked concerned, asking me if I wanted any food. I didn't say anything. I didn't want to lose my concentration, so I would shut my eyes again and go back to sleep, back to the memories. Five, four, three, two, one: I would count down and the visions would come when summoned.

There was a time I remember waking up, sunshine bright in my eyes. Someone had opened the shades and, when I focused, I felt Xander's presence. He was looking down with worry. Then he grinned when he saw my eyes flutter open. "You want anything to eat?" he asked. "Or maybe we could go play some video games? I'm tired of beating Roy." I didn't say anything; I just closed my eyes again. Five, four, three, two, one: Back to the memories.

I had no idea how long I was out, but I do know that when I awoke that last time, I knew what I had to do. It was dark out now and I could hear the snores from my friends, silent breathing from the twins, the rough rumble from Roy and the slight wheezing from Xander. I used my gifts to ease myself out of the room without a sound.

I was on the way out of the room with my flying helmet; anything else I could get along the way. But as I crept out, I suddenly realized I was starving. I had no idea how long I'd been sleeping, how long I'd been thinking, sifting through memories, but my stomach was grumbling and I knew I had to get something to eat before I left.

I slithered through the gloomy halls, half expecting to see someone. The lights were dim and no one else appeared. By the time I got to the cafeteria, I hoped maybe I'd make a clean break so that no one would stand in my way and there would be no witnesses. I'd like it better that way. I was half-way through stuffing Power Bars, granola bars and a couple water bottles in my pocket when I heard something from the back of the kitchen. I tried to slip back out the way I'd come, but there he was: Kennedy. All gray hair and perfectly tanned skin, he strolled out in his pajamas with a bowl and a box of Fruity Pebbles.

"I didn't think I would have any company," he said in a slightly British accent. "Would you like to join me, Benjamin?"

I'd been a little distant from him since the Destruction started. He was my first mentor after all, but I had changed. Obviously I had changed. Something about his little lessons bugged my teenage self. Don't get me wrong—I liked Kennedy; he was a great guy. He had some amazing stories and he'd seen a lot of things, but—. Maybe I'll just blame my resistance on being a teenager. I didn't really want to listen to adults right now. It just was not what I wanted.

"What? No, I was just grabbing some things for tomorrow morning."

"Early start?" he asked.

"Yeah, kind of. There was somebody we were going to look for tomorrow. Turns out it's pretty close by, so we lucked out."

"I hadn't heard," he said taking a seat and pouring the Fruity Pebbles over the milk in his bowl. He always like to do things a little bit backwards. "Come Benjamin, have a seat with me. Let's chat."

Oh, man. Talk about self-control. It took every ounce I had not to roll my eyes, but I willed my impatience down as I took a seat across from Kennedy. I pulled a granola bar out of my pocket. I was already through one granola bar and reaching for another before he said anything else.

I really was starving. My stomach kept begging for more food. What I really wanted was some bacon and eggs, maybe some pancakes, maybe some French toast too, with a ton of butter and syrup. That's what I really wanted. I had to make do with the granola bars that I'd stuffed in my pockets.

"Are you really going on a recruiting mission, Benjamin?" he asked, shoveling another heaping teaspoon of cereal into his mouth. I didn't want to lie to him; besides, I was a terrible liar. Everybody knew it when I lied, or at least when I tried to.

"I need to get away by myself." *There, I'd said it.* I hadn't told him everything, but I'd said what I needed to. Kennedy cocked his head and stared at me with those gleaming blue eyes that always reminded me of some sky blue ocean in some tropical place.

"How are you doing, Benjamin? I'm sorry I haven't asked, but we've all been busy, haven't we?" I nodded. Everybody had a job, even the youngest of the gifted known as The Keepers had responsibilities. Most days it seemed like there were too few of us. That's why we had to keep recruiting. We needed more.

"How are you handling your mother's absence?" he asked. He was probing because he was my friend. He wanted to make sure I was okay. I was pretty sure from his tone that he didn't know the whole truth. Clearly my father hadn't told any of what he'd told me to anyone else.

"It's not easy," I said. "I miss her. I wish she were here, but I understand that she might need some time. I guess maybe that's why I need some time. Does that make sense?"

Kennedy gave me a slow nod. "Did I ever tell you that I was your age during World War II?"

"Yes."

"I was young, but I looked older than my age, though not as old as I look now, but I still looked older. When the queen asked for more troops, I went with them; I went with one of my brothers."

"Was he gifted too?" I asked. I'd never heard this story. Kennedy had all kinds of stories about recent times, lessons always intertwined with his talent, but I'd never heard about his earlier days. Despite my need to leave, I wanted to listen to his story.

"No, he was not gifted," Kennedy said. "I kept that a secret. You see, back in those days, we weren't as organized as we are today, but during and because of the war, many of us found each other. My brother and I thought it would be an adventure, and at first it was. I lied about my age, and we enlisted together in the army. We soon found ourselves fighting the Nazis.

It took all of two days on the front lines to realize that we'd miscalculated—that it wasn't an adventure—that it wasn't like playing in our backyard or at school. It was war, and it was real. Nobody ever tells you about the smell. Did you know that? It's hard to describe what war smells like. For me, the war smelled like smoke and burning, especially the burning bodies. We had to do that sometimes. It was filthy business, and then there was the smell of burning latrines."

Kennedy crinkled his nose at the memory. "Well, I'm sure you don't want to hear about that. It was hard not to use my gifts in those days, very hard. It would have been easy for me to fling all manner of projectiles at the enemy with pinpoint accuracy. I was good at that, but I was afraid of what would have happened. I was afraid that if they knew I had those powers they would either try to kill me or use me. You see, in those days, the Nazis especially looked for people with powers. They were very much interested in the supernatural as well. Adolf Hitler had special assets troops who scoured the globe for ancient relics. I was afraid I would become one of those relics—a living one—a weapon that they could use." I winced, but he didn't seem to notice. It reminded me of The Ancient and of my mother, weapons used against other people—human weapons.

Kennedy continued, "We fought our way through Africa, alongside Americans and against General Erwin Rommel on the German side. Those were long years but, somehow miraculously, my brother and I both survived. Eventually, our unit was redeployed to France. We stormed the beach along with the Americans on the D-Day landing in Normandy. If you could have seen that sight—it was quite amazing. There were so many ships, so many boats and so many men charging across the English Channel, taking the fight to the enemy. They were brave boys, so brave, but as you know, nothing comes easy in war. We lost many men, many of my friends, and on that day, I lost my brother. I cannot begin to tell you what pain that loss brought. It was like something reached inside my chest and tore out my heart.

"We'd been close before the war, but during the war our bond had grown so much stronger. Even though he was three years my senior, he still treated me as his equal, and I loved him for that. Now he was dead, his head resting on a sandy shore, eyes gazing up for eternity to the sky smeared with smoke – a black, black smoke. A switch flipped inside of me, and I left my unit. They call it AWOL now. Back then they called it desertion, but I didn't desert. I used my gifts, the ones that I'd been secretly practicing when no one was around.

"I waited until nightfall, and then I took to the sky. In my wake, I leveled ultimate destruction. I tore impregnable concrete bunkers from hillsides, crushing them, killing everyone inside. I flung whole squads of men into the air where they came crashing down. They would never fight again when they were dead, or barely living. And I went searching for my brother's killers. The Nazis were the only thing on my mind. I saw them as the purest enemy. By the time the sun rose the next day, I'd made it ten miles inland, tearing a jagged path into France.

"Later, there were reports of extraterrestrial activity, or some elite unit with some magical weapon that had done it, but it was me. It was another one of our kind that found me one hundred miles from our front lines in a barn that was half destroyed from Allied bombings. He wore the uniform of an army major. When I asked him how he'd found me, he didn't say. It was only later that he would tell me that The Mystics had told him how to find me. I was in full hysterics by that point from the stress of my brother's death and the horror of what I'd done. It all came crashing down on me. I didn't know how to handle it. Keith took me back to others like us.

"There were Healers, Growers, and more Destructors, as we called ourselves at the time. It took a week of praying, thinking and conversing with those wonderful people before I realized that it wasn't my fault. That American major explained they'd all been through similar circumstances and loss. At that point, they were trying to save people, so I joined them.

"There were times when we did have to fight the enemy—when a certain situation presented itself and we had to protect our side—the Allies or one of our members, but mostly we traveled helping others. The Healers helped the wounded, the Growers used their talents to spring orchards from the earth and lead displaced civilians to their sanctuary for food and comfort. I was particularly adept at finding survivors in the rubble of bombings or shelling. I stopped counting after I saved two hundred. After that it didn't really matter.

"I tell you all this, Benjamin, because I know how you feel. I know the loss that stabs at you. I know how it can grip your soul and threaten your very lifeblood, but I also know the importance of looking at the good in things, the bright side, if you will. I won't ask where you're going. I know you're responsible and will take care of yourself. I know you'll think things through, but I will tell you that there are those here who love you, trust you and hope that you find the answers you're looking for."

CHAPTER 12

Xander's Log

Well, it looks like he's really gone. Man—I'll tell you what—of anyone I ever thought would run away, I never thought it was going to be ol' Benjamin. That kid—whew—he snuck out in the middle of the night and nobody saw him. Well, at least according to the rumor mill. We know they've got cameras up in this place, and I'll bet somebody knows when he left.

But the thing that stinks now is—well—a few things stink. First, they want us to do these stupid journals, these log books, like they're talking about. Pretty lame if you ask me. I know what they're doing. They keep asking us to write about Benjamin, about what we saw him do, what we heard him say. But you know what? I'm not a snitch. Oh, and if you're reading this, know that I'm going to break out of here as soon as I can—I'm out.

Roy's Log

Testing…testing. Knock, knock, knock. I'm not sure if I'm using this thing right. Lily showed me, but I'm too worried about Benjamin to focus. His dad said he doesn't know where he is. Benjamin didn't tell us he was leaving. He slept for three days—I mean three entire days. Then he just up and disappeared in the middle of the night. I'm worried that he's going to look for this voice by himself.

I thought he would have learned that lesson a long time ago. Why did he go off alone? I would have helped him. We all would have helped him. Even Xander's mad that Benjamin left him behind. I hope he calls soon. I hope he checks in. He left his cell phone behind, but that doesn't mean he can't call us from another phone. I'd better go. I need to get some food. Okay, how do I turn this thing off? Knock, knock, knock.

Jasmine's Log

I don't care what you people think. I'm leaving; I'm done with this. You think you can keep us here just because Benjamin ran away? Well, I'm not your slave. This isn't a prison; it's supposed to be our home. But now you're making us do these stupid logs. Lily and Roy, well—I'm leaving. Don't try to find me.

Lily's Log

I can't believe she left. My sister *left*. What was she thinking? I can't say that I'm surprised. I'm just hurt, I guess. I can't believe she didn't tell me. She probably didn't tell me because she knows I'd try to convince her to stay. She's been mad. Mad at me—mad at Roy. I can't help my feelings. What was I supposed to do? Not talk to Roy because Jasmine wanted me to herself? Well that's not just stupid; it's completely childish. We are fifteen now. But to make things worse, she took Xander with her.

I guess that's good because neither of them will be alone, unlike Benjamin. I've got Roy, and that's great and all, but all he does is spend his days worrying about Benjamin and where he could have gone. Sometimes we don't talk for hours, even though we're in the same room. I wish I could do something. I wish I could say something to make him feel better, like 'It isn't your fault.' But that's Roy, he won't believe it. He thinks Benjamin is his responsibility, but he's not. Benjamin was all of our responsibility, but really Benjamin is his own responsibility. We can't tell him what to do. He's the best of us. I know that—even Xander knows that.

But I think there's something more to Benjamin leaving. I think he's trying to keep the rest of us safe, and something tells me he's not worried about his own safety. Yeah, I kind of agree with Roy that maybe Benjamin's being a little too reckless this time. But who am I to judge? I'm not his mom. I just hope he contacts us soon, at least for Roy's peace of mind.

Roy's Log

Mr. Dragon, I wanted to tell you face-to-face that we're leaving, but you're not here. The other adults said that you've left. I'm leaving you this message in my log. Lily and I are going; we have to. We'll try to stay in touch. Lily says that if we bring her computer, we can keep doing this log thing, but I'm not sure. I'm really not sure where we're going. I'm sorry I can't tell you that; I really am. But we need to get out of here. If Benjamin comes back, let him hear this. Tell him I'm sorry that he didn't trust me enough to tell me what he was doing or where he was going. If he ever asks me, I'll tell him exactly where I am. Good-bye, Mr. Dragon. I hope to see you soon.

CHAPTER 13

Part II

Things quieted down for a time at the Lake Como complex. There had never been any regularity of down-times between disasters, but for some reason this felt different, like The Destructors were taking a time-out to regroup. So life went on like it always did with The Keepers' training and digging new paths through their mountains. However, some took this rare opportunity to visit their families all over the world.

It was no secret that Benjamin and his friends had disappeared. Some whispered that they were on a secret mission cut off from all methods of communication. Others said that the five friends had had a falling out. There was no real evidence supporting this, but that didn't stop the rumors. What everybody did know was that without Benjamin's visions, all recruitment had stopped. While this had come as a surprise to most, after a while it felt like a weight had been lifted from their shoulders. It had been a long five years for everyone. The constant threat looming just over the horizon was hard to live with, even when you were surrounded by people with powers, with gifts that let them do extraordinary things.

During Benjamin's absence, a strange thing occurred—something that even the oldest among them felt a little bad about, their consciences not quite clear. They would never say it aloud—although many thought it privately—but they were glad that Benjamin was gone. It meant their workload and stress levels were lessened. Deep down, in their darkest thoughts, some actually believed that maybe Benjamin had been tied to the destruction, because after all, it had ceased when Benjamin left Lake Como. It would take a tidal wave of The Destructors to convince anyone to admit it aloud, but like a tiny mouse left to its own devices in an old, rickety barn, the idea grew and festered, multiplying as one idea joined another and then another, until the fuller picture was formed.

In the end, no one really knew the truth. Even Benjamin's father didn't know it all, but it wasn't like he would say anything. He was rarely at the mansion anyway. He'd made himself scarce as well after Benjamin's departure, leaving on frequent trips.

There were two Keepers remaining who were concerned about young Benjamin. They'd been the first to meet the young boy at the age of ten: Kennedy, Benjamin's first assigned mentor, and Wally Goodfriend, the giant of a man whose healing gifts were especially treasured. Late one night, the two men sat on the portico of the mansion overlooking Lake Como. The stars dotted the sky overhead, not twinkling, just observing from on high. The half-moon cast its gaze over them in white luminescence, echoing ripples across the water.

"Do you think he's all right?" Wally asked his friend, sipping from an enormous mug of homemade hot chocolate, one of his specialties.

Kennedy didn't answer at first, too busy fishing out one of the handful of marshmallows he'd deposited in his own hot chocolate. When he finally snagged one and plopped it in his mouth he answered, "I have faith in our young Benjamin. He'll find his way soon enough."

Wally's face made it plain he wasn't as convinced. The man's big heart felt for young Benjamin. He wanted him to be nearby and safe, but he knew Kennedy was probably right; Kennedy was usually right. Benjamin wasn't a little boy anymore. He could take care of himself. He didn't need Wally or Kennedy watching over his shoulder, instructing him what to do or what not to do. However, he still feared for his young friend's safety and wellbeing.

"Have you heard anything from the others?" Wally implored, in reference to Benjamin's four friends.

Kennedy shook his head. "We have the new boy, Francis, helping track them. He's rather adept with computers, you know."

Wally smiled. Despite looking like a mountain man, Wally was very comfortable around technology. He and Francis had bonded over their love of computers and technology. While Wally found he had little to teach him, Francis had taught Wally plenty, finding an apt pupil in the giant man.

Then Wally frowned again, "It's been months, Kennedy. You don't think we should go look for him?"

"I do not," Kennedy answered with firm resolution, "He will reach out in time. I have faith in that. We can't pressure him. We just have to trust him."

Wally noted, with trepidation, Kennedy had been careful to say "reach out" and not that Benjamin was returning home. He hoped that wasn't the case. The mansion and training facilities were much too quiet without Benjamin and his companions. Wally could only hope that Kennedy was somehow wrong and that Benjamin would make his way home soon.

CHAPTER 14

Francis took off his coke-bottle glasses and rubbed his eyes. He had been at it too long and things were starting to blur. His eyes and hands ached from working at the computer so long. He would rather be training in the caverns beneath the mountains with the other kids, but he knew what he was doing was important; they had to find Benjamin.

He had not known him long, but Francis knew Benjamin was different, someone special. He was a natural leader, even though he never acted like it. Kind of like one of those people who don't know what their abilities are. That was what he noticed about Benjamin. The way the others, even the big kid, Roy Birch, followed him without question.

Part of Francis envied Benjamin for that innate ability. It was something that Francis had never had. Maybe it came with being smart or maybe it just came with being in a wheelchair and looking the way he did, but he did envy Benjamin. Maybe that had a little bit to do with the hours he had put into the search. He had never been the shining trophy for his parents to hold up and say, "Look world, look at what we made," but something in Francis told him that if he found Benjamin, he might share part of that spotlight.

All his work was not just self-serving. He was curious and, for as long as he could remember, was enamored by the secrets computers held. This curiosity was one of the reasons he had gotten so good with computers. He had learned to code at the age of six, not because he had to, but because he wanted to know how it worked. He'd wanted to know how those lines of gibberish could somehow spout out a HD video game. He had even written some himself until he got bored. The thing about Francis was that if he wasn't challenged, he moved on. He knew he could have been some kind of prodigy if he'd stuck to one thing, but that was boring. He did always come back to computers. The technology of a computer was like a present with layers that you kept unwrapping yet you never got to the center of it. Francis viewed it as the most wondrous tool he had ever beheld. Now, with the resources of The Keepers, Francis was at the forefront of the search.

That was one of the cool things about being at the mansion. The adults did not really treat the kids like kids. It was the first time in his life that had happened and he appreciated it. Most everyone was nice, but everybody was respectful. At first, he had wondered if that was just because everybody had gifts. He thought It might be especially true if you could move things with your mind, as if maybe you were a danger. He had assumed that, "Hey, they're being nice to me because they think that maybe I'll do something bad." He quickly come to learn that was not it at all. Instead these people, the ones who called themselves The Keepers, that he was now a part of, all lived with mutual respect.

Over the months, Francis had quickly come to understand and share that same feeling. Nobody looked at him like he was a freak here. Sure, there had been curious stares at first, but when the other kids, and even the adults, found out he could fix pretty much anything with wires or memory chips, his physical handicap had been forgotten. The smart mouth that he had always been so famous for with the kids in school in California or even with his parents soon went away. Although his biting wit never truly disappeared, they liked him for that here. They respected him for it. The other Keepers liked that he was smart, that he contributed in his own special way. For Francis, that beat everything else. He was finally accepted; he was finally at home. He replaced his glasses in the notch on the bridge of his nose, sniffed once, cracked his knuckles, and went back to work. It was just past midnight, but he knew he could manage a couple more hours of work before exhaustion took him.

At some time past three in the morning, an alert popped up on the computer screen. Francis glanced at it, ready to ignore it and get back to what he had just been doing, but his fingers stopped. His eyes hovered over the new data. He had written a simple program to scour the Internet for forums and social media groups that discussed anything from paranormal activity to some kind of wondrous event. Some were religious in nature and others were downright weird. There were a lot of bizarre things that people were into these days. It had taken a solid three days of fine tuning to get the program streamlined enough to work the way he wanted. Now, instead of getting one hundred alerts an hour, he was getting maybe one or two.

Every alert, up until that moment, he had ignored, but this one was different. The title was what got him. It was a new thread in a forum somewhere in Indonesia and the new thread was simply titled, "My Guardian Angel." The body of the message was written in that formal second language so familiar in countries like Indonesia and India. The message was brief, but to the point.

"Walking to the university today, I had a near-death experience. A bus filled with too many people approached me from the other direction. The driver saw me, but it was too late. I could not move out of the way and he could not turn. I should not have been texting on my phone, stupid phone. When I looked up, I saw his eyes wide just like mine. His mouth opened, screaming most likely. I had no time to scream. I knew I was going to die, but before I could say a prayer, the bus was lifted straight up into the air. Tires were spinning and throwing mud from the dirty road. Nothing touched me except for the mud that rained down on my head.

I collapsed to my knees as the bus moved over my head, settled down, and went on its way. The driver did not stop. Perhaps he thought it was a dream. I know it was not a dream for when I looked up into the sky, there was only the bright shining sun, but when I looked to the road, there was another—someone not of our town. Someone I had never seen before with fair skin and blue jeans. He waved once, smiled and disappeared into the jungle. I do not know who you are, guardian angel, but I say thank you and God bless you."

Francis read the passage "fair skin, dark jeans, a wave and a smile" three times. It might have sounded ridiculous to anyone else, but to Francis it sounded like an exact description of Benjamin. He bookmarked the thread and promised to return to it later. The first-hand account had energized him. He was ready to go back to work, but just as he closed the box on the screen another appeared. It was an alert, the same as the last one.

This one was in reply to the first message, "Did he have dark hair?"

The originator of the post replied not long after, "Yes, dark hair, short, but not too short."

The second person messaged back a moment later: "I think I encountered the same person. I was swimming last night in the ocean, but the tide took me out too far. With a net of fishes I had gathered, it weighed me down. Even when I tried to cast the net aside, I could not swim ashore. I had picked a lonely beach where no one else was, so if I had yelled, no one would have heard me, and so I prayed. When I did, I was lifted from the water. When whatever power set me on the beach, my legs were shaking with relief. I believe I saw the same person as you. He waved, smiled, and then disappeared. I am also in Indonesia. Has anyone else seen the same?"

Francis waited. There were no more replies. Maybe it was a fluke, but then again maybe not. He should tell someone, but who? He had been assigned by Kennedy personally to work on the search. No one except for Benjamin's own dad knew what Francis was really doing, so Francis decided to sit on the information, and wait and see if more sightings occurred. Maybe this would just be the first of many, but then again maybe not. Francis yawned despite the fact that his mind was blazing. It could wait until morning, so he logged off the network and made his way to bed.

CHAPTER 15

Francis knew he should have set his alarm clock. By the time he woke up and peeked out the window, the sun was almost directly overhead. He hurried as best he could to get ready because he was anxious to get back to the computers. For some reason, everything was centralized and nobody was allowed to have a computer in any room but the lab. Francis understood that it probably had something to do with security and safety—that they wanted to keep all incoming and outgoing messages secure.

But part of it had sort of a socialist feel to it, like some governments try to control information shared. Francis understood it as a necessary security measure. His dad had been in the data protection business and developed security systems from the ground up as a business. Along the way, Francis had learned what proper Internet security measures really took. It wasn't easy, and unless you controlled access from a central location, it wasn't very hard for outside forces to hack their way in.

While the rest of the world had Wi-Fi, The Keepers had an old school computer lab. Well, not so old school—they did have the newest technology and that was uber-cool. The icing on the cake for Francis was he got to go inside where nobody else got to go. Because of his background and his talents, he was allowed to go inside the inner sanctum to work on the most crucial security apparatus The Keepers had. It was his home within a home, and he'd earned his own place at the table.

When he finally left his room, hair wet from how he'd combed it, it wasn't the usual morning Francis had expected. The usual passersby with their casual conversations were replaced by a hustle and bustle he had not seen before. The first thing he thought was that there had been another catastrophe, that The Destructors had struck again. He propelled his wheelchair faster, soon arriving at the bank of elevators at the end of the hall.

By the time he entered the Central Security office of The Keepers, Francis knew that it wasn't an attack. He'd overheard the whispers, and when he entered the office he saw video from all over the world. Newscasters were talking about some mysterious being, some kind of guardian angel who, according to initial reports, first appeared in Indonesia and then skipped to the Philippines. Francis attempted, to no avail, to get the attention of one of the adults, but everybody seemed to be either on the phone, or scrolling through the endless logs on their computers, sifting through videos, or sending emails to who knew where.

He logged onto his own computer, ignoring everyone else. When he did there were more than thirty alerts on his screen. There were some claims that sounded ridiculous, even to Francis, who knew there were people with gifts all over the world. He quickly discarded those, sifting through the messages. It started in Indonesia, just outside of Jakarta with the guy saved from the flying bus, then the one saved from the ocean and then there was an attack in the city of Jakarta itself. A woman had been saved from three men with knives.

Then there seemed to be a lull. The timestamps showed no more events for six hours before the next sighting. Then there was a new alert from the Philippines. Francis did a quick search to determine how long it took to fly from Jakarta to Manila, Philippines—four hours. He glanced at the timestamps. Yeah, that was about right.

As if on cue, he heard one of the adults talking loudly into a phone. "Yes, sir, we have him on a private flight from Jakarta to Manila. Should we close his account, sir?" The answer on the other end must have been *"No"* because the person in the office with Francis didn't move. He just hung up the phone and went back to whatever he had been doing.

Francis went back to his own work, scrolling through the messages mostly from young people in the Philippines. There was even a grainy photograph that someone had taken with her phone. It matched the earlier description as well as all the others. Now Francis didn't have a doubt—not that he really did before—it had to be Benjamin. What was he doing, and why was he doing it?

Timothy Dragon paced back and forth like he was General George Patton. Kennedy had known Benjamin's father for years, respected him and was proud to call him a friend. As he observed the man stomping around while in deep contemplation, it was hard to ignore the shoulder blades protruding from the man's shirt, like skeletal armor. To say Timothy's health had declined would be a gross understatement. First he had endured his wife leaving and then Benjamin disappearing. The stress had taken its toll, and anyone who didn't know him might assume that Timothy Dragon was sick with some terminal disease. Kennedy knew the truth of it—the man's heart was broken. He was upset, and he didn't know how to deal with it. The pain tore at him from the inside, like a ravaging bug that had somehow found its way inside him. It seemed to be a parasite so insidious the man harboring it didn't even know it was there, much less what it was.

Kennedy had been through multiple wars, the second World War being his first time in theater. He had been drawn to wars, both for the adventure and for the opportunity to help others. He had seen other leaders go through the same transformations as Timothy Dragon. He wanted to offer his assistance, to say something reassuring, but all he could do was sit there and wait. He knew it would take time; he would be there for his friend.

Finally, Benjamin's father spoke, "This can't be a coincidence. It has to be Benjamin. First sighted in Indonesia and now they're telling me the Philippines. They've even confirmed that Benjamin was on a private flight to the Philippines. Now he's probably headed somewhere like Hawaii, although we don't know the precise location. Tell me, why shouldn't I put a hold on his account?"

Kennedy mulled over the question. It was a valid one. If he were Benjamin's father, he might be tempted to do likewise and send out a search party to bring Benjamin back to safety. However, Kennedy had the luxury of being outside that familial circle and could offer the voice of objectivity.

"I think we should wait to see where he's headed and what he's up to." Timothy shot a murderous glare at Kennedy, his eyes softening only after he realized how he was acting. It took visible effort. He exhaled sharply and then inhaled like a whip. "He's *my son*, Kennedy. He's all I have left. I need to get him back. Can't you see that? Why can't you understand?"

Kennedy had never had children. He had never been married, but he had lost many who had been close to him. He knew love, and he knew loss. He answered with his own question, "How do we know that Benjamin hasn't seen something—something to make him act the way he has?"

Timothy Dragon actually growled this time, "Can't you see what a mistake he's making? He's exposing himself to the world. But not just himself—he's exposing us. Jacee and his goons already have us cornered, and now Benjamin is helping them."

Kennedy wasn't so sure and he told Timothy so. "I truly believe that Benjamin has our wellbeing foremost in his mind. Let us not forget who he is and the miraculous gifts that he's been given."

Timothy wouldn't be convinced. He shook his head in silent disagreement. "Has there been any word from the others? From Roy, Lily, Jasmine or Xander?" he asked.

"Not that I'm aware of," Kennedy answered.

"Do you think they're helping him? Do you think they know what he's up to or where he is?"

Kennedy sighed. This conversation was going nowhere. Timothy was obviously anxiety ridden, and there was some truth to what he was saying. While he was in this frame of mind, however, it was best to go along with him until intervention was needed. Timothy was, after all, the appointed administrator of The Keepers.

"Benjamin might be our de facto leader, but he's never had any role in the day-to-day operations of the Lake Como chateau. Why don't I talk to the new boy, Francis? Perhaps he has some leads on what Benjamin's up to. I bet my left foot that Francis has been monitoring the situation online. Why don't you let me have a conversation with him? Then I'll let you know what he says." Timothy Dragon nodded his consent, his eyes glazed over and he returned to his pacing.

Kennedy had located Francis in the Central Security office. They had tucked him away in a little corner, thinking he needed privacy. It didn't seem to bother Francis one bit. Kennedy still wasn't sure what to make of the boy in the wheelchair. He was bright enough. He had his talents, and his gifts seemed to be growing more each day. His instructors, when he had time for instruction, said he was quickly grasping everything he was taught. That didn't surprise Kennedy. Oh boy, with his background, he was sure to have focus. He'd only had brief conversations with the boy, but he sensed there was more to Francis than you could see with the naked eye.

"Francis, I was wondering if I could have a word with you?" Kennedy asked.

Francis put up a finger like he was finishing something up. It was a full thirty seconds before he finally turned. "Oh, Mr. Kennedy, I'm sorry. I didn't know it was you. I thought it was one of the others."

He didn't sound sorry, more like he'd been taught it was good manners, and he was vaguely worried about saying the right thing. Kennedy smiled, "Why don't we go to the conference room? There's a little more privacy there." Kennedy watched the boy as he wheeled over and positioned his chair on the opposite side of the conference room table.

While other children his age might have been concerned about being called into a private meeting, Francis didn't appear to be shaken in the least. "How have you been getting along with the others?" Kennedy asked.

"Oh, just fine, you know. I've been kind of busy down here, but when I get the chance to be with the others, everybody's pretty cool."

"And your lessons—have you made time for them?"

Francis nodded. He had an almost bored look on his face. "Yeah, like I said, they keep me pretty busy down here, and well, there's a lot to look for with Benjamin being gone and all. But when I can, I make the time."

The boy didn't seem overly concerned, and to be quite honest Kennedy wasn't either. Not every one of The Keepers had to have matching gifts. What he wanted now was to see what Francis's technological savvy might have produced. "I assume you've been monitoring the latest situation online?" Kennedy asked.

For the first time Francis seemed interested. He leaned forward in his chair to rest his hands on the table, much like a consultant or a CEO might. The boy's presence changed; he was all business now. "What do you want to know?" Francis countered.

"I'd like to know what you think. What's your take on the situation?"

Francis pursed his lips. "Are you asking whether I think it's Benjamin or—?"

Kennedy shook his head and grinned. "I think we all know it's Benjamin. I'd like to know what you think about it. What do you think Benjamin is doing? What is the purpose of him revealing himself to so many people in such a short time?"

Francis actually stroked his chin, the way Kennedy assumed Socrates might have before he dictated some profound passage. "I don't have anything concrete, you understand. It's just, well, I think my gut's telling me something."

Kennedy nodded, "That's all I'm asking for. Give me your honest assessment. You see, some others are concerned about what Benjamin is doing. They're worried that he's putting himself and us at risk. Do you think that's his intent?"

Francis snorted, "Mr. Kennedy—look—I have no idea what the general situation is with The Keepers and this complex. They have me monitor the Internet and help in any way I can. Nobody's ever really told me what our mission is or what we actually do. If you're asking if he's somehow compromising what we're trying to do here, I have no idea. But if you are asking me whether I think he's doing something specifically, then yeah, I might have a hunch or two."

Now they were getting somewhere, Kennedy thought. "What would that hunch be, Francis? What does your intuition tell you that Benjamin is doing?"

Francis adjusted himself in his wheelchair. "Look, people do things for all kinds of reasons. Some people are crazy. Others just don't know what's going on, and I really didn't know Benjamin for long. But there's an obvious pattern here. You might think that maybe he's off on an adventure, but I think it's something more. I think he's got a plan, and I don't think he wants to tell us what that plan is yet."

"And if you had to guess, what do you think Benjamin's plan is?"

Francis smiled like he was in on a secret. "Something that only you and he might know. I think he's trying to send a message."

"What kind of message?" Kennedy asked.

Francis tapped his temple with one index finger before responding, "That's exactly what I'm trying to ferret out."

CHAPTER 16

Xander fought the urge to close his eyes and take a nap on the bench. In a few minutes he'd be able to go into the hotel room and take a nap there. In truth, he could sleep pretty much anywhere, but a bed sounded much more comfortable than a park bench. He yawned aloud, and a moment later Jasmine exited the hotel lobby. She crossed the street and flashed two key cards in the air. One of the perks of being a Keeper was they had fake IDs and fake names, so when it came to traveling on the road they could stay in pretty much any hotel. Xander still preferred Jasmine to go in and make the reservations; she could charm the socks off a beggar—if she wanted to.

Jasmine flipped Xander one of the access cards. He caught it in his left hand. "Room 207," she said. "Meet me up there in five minutes." It was their usual routine; it was better not to go in together. People thought it was weird. It wasn't as if they looked like siblings or anything.

"Please tell me you got two beds," Xander teased. Jasmine gave him an annoyed look, as if to say she would never think of sharing a single bed with him. She turned and went back into the hotel. Xander glanced at his watch and noted the time. Five minutes later, he casually strolled through the same hotel lobby.

It wasn't anything fancy, but it was clean. It smelled like fresh flowers. He walked by the meager bar, past a bored barmaid who was wiping the top of the wood in slow and measured strokes. It seemed she thought her slow motion cleaning would take more time and make her workday fly faster. Xander was about to head to the elevators when he noticed a TV screen above the barmaid's head. "Excuse me, could you turn that up please?" he asked. She looked up, not annoyed, just bored, and then turned around slowly to adjust the volume.

"BBC reporting from Trevane International. Today I'm happy to be talking with Mr. Jacee Trevane, whose foundation has independently saved many of the world's population. Once a pop culture icon, he has quickly become one of the most influential people on the planet. Mr. Trevane, thank you so much for meeting with me today."

"It's my pleasure, and please call me Jacee."

The female reporter nodded and Trevane gave her a little smile. "Now Jacee, I'm sure the entire world would like to know why you dedicate so much time and money to this cause."

He flashed that famous Jacee Trevane smile, the one the whole world knew by now. "First, let me clarify that it is my foundation, and the people who work within it, dedicating time and money to this cause. I am not acting alone. We feel compelled to serve others and thus carry out our mission to assist those less unfortunate. I suppose you could say it's a calling.

"We can't be sure why the massive devastation has happened in the manner it has, or even where the devastation has come from, although I do have my own thoughts regarding this matter. But our mission at Trevane International is to help those affected. We provide food, shelter and counseling. Most recently we've met with world leaders to begin the process of relocating thousands of displaced citizens. It's not an overnight thing, but I'm hoping, by the end of the year, to make great strides in building new welcoming communities for these homeless refugees."

"I'm sorry, Jacee, you said you have some thoughts on why this is happening. This is the first you've mentioned it—" Jacee shrugged, like he didn't want to say. Xander moved one step closer to the television. "I'm not quite sure this is the correct forum to share my information with—"

"Please, we'd love to know your thoughts. I'm sure most of the world would agree that you've earned the right to share your opinions."

After a calculating nod, Jacee began, "I'll preface this by saying I have no proof of what I'm about to say. I have my people looking into it, of course, but what if this has all been some type of new beginning? What if it has always been the destiny of all mankind for these unfortunate and life-altering events to occur? We, as a global entity, have made many choices that might have led to this event. What if this was the universe's way of saying we did it wrong? That we need to make better decisions—that we need to come together. What if that's true?"

"I'm not sure I follow your meaning. Are you saying that this is some sort of religious awakening? Because if you are, wouldn't that only fuel the flames of religious discontent? We've seen Christians fighting Muslims over this. Atheists are condemning believers. Now you're saying that it might be true? I'm sorry, Mr. Trevane, but I find this a little hard to believe."

He gave the reporter a patient nod. "Why would that be so outlandish? Because we can't see it or touch it? I've believed for some time that there's a certain spiritual current that runs through us all that provides us the will to live. It is this current that bands us together in times of need, and when the world is at its worst that current pushes back. Think of what was happening five years ago—war in the Middle East, hunger in Africa, and political battles raged for no other reason than to make the opposing sides feel better about themselves. But now, look, it might not be easy to see, but it's there; I feel it. People are starting to work together and come together as one, grasping the hope that we *can* prevail." Then Trevane shook his head like he just realized what he was saying. "I'm sorry, I know this all sounds bizarre, medieval really, but it's what I believe and I can't change that. I hope you understand."

Xander wished in that moment that he could understand what Jacee was really up to. He'd had his own dealings with Jacee, and he knew the man always had a motive behind every action. To Xander's surprise, the reporter did not let Jacee off easy, or at least not as easily as one might have expected.

"Mr. Trevane, could you tell me your thoughts on the recent reports of the mystery man, or guardian angel if you wish, who has been spotted in Indonesia and the Philippines? The one rumored to be moving toward the United States?"

There it was—the briefest flicker—but Xander saw it. You had to know Jacee to catch it and Xander did. There was annoyance, even a little anger, but it snapped away with another flashy smile.

"I've heard the stories and they do sound incredible," Trevane said. "I really do hope that they are true, and I'm happy for those who've been helped, but let's not forget the people who've been on the ground for five years—my friends and coworkers at Trevane International, have saved thousands. Those are the people we should be thanking and talking about. Not this guardian angel, not even me, but the good people toiling hard every day to help the needy. Now, if you don't mind, we have a very busy day planned."

The reporter nodded and turned back to the camera, "And there you have it, Mr. Jacee Trevane, founder of Trevane International."

Xander grinned and shook his head. Maybe that's what Benjamin's disappearance was all about. Maybe he was trying to get under Trevane's skin. Xander had to admire him for that. The only thing he wished was that he could be helping him do it and that gave him an idea. He'd have to talk to Jasmine about it; she'd have to be on board but he didn't think that'd be a problem. Xander hurried from the lobby and rushed up to the room.

Jasmine watched the recap of the brief interview with a straight face, like she always did. It was rare for her to display emotion, which sometimes ticked Xander off. Most times he respected her calm. It meant that she rarely got unraveled, and that's what made it so surprising when she almost strangled Francis. When he laid out his ideas and plans about what he thought they should do, he was once again surprised to see her smile. "I think you're onto something," she said, "Now, if only we could tell Lily and Roy the same thing."

Roy and Lily walked hand in hand down the dusty dirt road, swirls of gravel mist marked their passing. It was hot but neither seemed to care. "I really like your parents," Lily said, "Your mom's sweet."

Roy gave Lily's hand a little squeeze. "I think they really like you," he said.

"I didn't know what they would say," she squeezed his hand back. "and now I know why you're so tall. Your dad's huge."

Roy chuckled, "Yeah, they make them big in my family".

"Do you think they're still buying your story that you are away at horse camp?"

When Roy first left home, after Kennedy found him, they told the Birches that Roy was going to an elite horse training facility. They'd maintained the same story ever since, but Roy was pretty sure that his parents didn't believe it anymore. While he didn't like lying to his parents, he knew he couldn't tell them the truth. They were superstitious in their own way, and the revelation that their son had some type of unnatural powers might lead to them think differently about their son. That was the last thing that Roy wanted.

"Yeah, I'm sure they think that something else is going on but, just between us, I don't think they want to know the truth. They're just overjoyed to see me happy." Roy shrugged, "I don't know if that makes any sense."

"It does. Sometimes parents believe that whole *ignorance is bliss* thing. I think it makes them feel better about either having made the right decision by us or that they didn't mess up too bad when they were raising us."

Roy nodded. He truly appreciated how insightful Lily was with most things. She had the intuition of someone much older, and that was one of the many reasons that Roy was enchanted by her. She was also one of the most beautiful beings he'd ever seen. He found most days all he did was think about her.

They had their first disagreement soon after leaving the mansion. She politely accused him of being too overprotective. He explained that he honestly didn't know what that meant; he was just being himself. However, when she explained how it seemed from her side, he understood. He'd been raised to protect anything/anyone that he loved. As sure as there was a sun in the sky, he loved Lily, so he tried every day not to smother her. It helped to know that Lily wasn't defenseless on her own. Besides Benjamin, Lily and her sister were probably the best of the five on offense. They were like silent spiders that could sneak on the attack and retreat just as quickly.

"What do you think about what your mom said?" Lily asked. "Would it be better if I got a hotel room maybe in town?"

"Mom would be offended, besides you can choose between the guestroom upstairs or you can take my room. It's your choice; it doesn't matter to me."

"No, you take your room. It's been a long time since you've been in there anyway, hasn't it?

"Yeah, I can't believe it's been five years–more really."

"Do you miss it?" Lily asked.

"I miss my parents. I miss my mom's food. She makes these biscuits that warm your belly and tickle your toes—at least that's what my dad always says. So yeah, I miss that kind of stuff, but I don't miss the life. I know my life belongs with you, Benjamin, Jasmine and even Xander." They rarely talked of home, probably because everyone's home was so different. Xander didn't even have one. Both of his parents were dead, so it was easier to avoid the topic of home. For some of the group, it was a sore subject.

"What about you? Do you miss staying at your dad's place?"

Lily shook her head.

"We FaceTime. Jasmine and I have seen him a couple of times over the years; you remember: you were there once. His place in San Diego is, well, not really my style." Roy knew what she was really alluding to. It wasn't the place or even the city. It was the young wife that their father had married. Roy didn't ask, but he bet she was no older than twenty-five. She had the look of one of those girls who had tried to be an actress, had never quite made it, but instead she found a guy with a lot of money and settled.

"What about Jasmine? Does she feel the same way?"

Lily shrugged. "I guess—I mean—we don't really talk about it, you know."

"Well, at least now we know if you ever want a home-cooked meal, my parents will be happy to have you," he said. She looked up at him and smiled, one of those grateful smiles like he had said exactly what she needed to hear at that exact moment. The look made him flush, and he had to turn away so he wouldn't get too embarrassed.

"Do you think we should head back?" Lily asked, wrapping her arm around his waist. She nestled in against his side, despite the blazing heat.

He wanted her to never let go. Roy wasn't ready to go back to the house. They had things to discuss. "Do you think it's time to go back to Italy? I mean, they must know something about where Benjamin is by now." He and Lily had heard the rumors, the ones about the kid showing up to save people. Both knew that it had to be Benjamin and both wondered about his actions the same as the others. They'd talked about it late into each night with Lily doing more speculating than Roy. Oh, he had his own thoughts on the subject. He just liked to hear her talk, with her almost melodic voice rattling off hypothesis after hypothesis.

"I think we should stay here a couple days, if that's okay with you. I'm sure your parents enjoy having you home."

"They do," he said, but the pit of his stomach told him that if he stayed he'd become restless. It was the protector in him–the Praetor. They'd been trying to sniff out Benjamin's trail with no success, and it'd been a last minute decision to swing through Texas to visit Roy's parents. While he was glad to see them, he knew he had a duty to attend to. He had a responsibility, not only to The Keepers, but also to Benjamin, Lily, Jasmine and Xander. "Maybe we stay the night," he said, "and see what the morning brings."

Lily didn't argue. She knew him. She knew once Roy had set his mind on something he would see it through. Instead of pressing, she asked, "Do you think your mom is going to make some of those biscuits tonight?"

After being stuffed full of chicken fried steak, Texas barbecue and gravy-smothered biscuits, Roy and Lily went out into the night, now thankfully twenty degrees cooler. Lily powered up her laptop and they watched a replay of the same interview Jasmine and Xander had seen hours earlier. "I *really* don't like that guy," Lily said, her arms crossed over her chest, her disapproval of Jacee Trevane palpable.

"I wish we knew what he was up to," Roy lamented, "but I bet Benjamin knows." Lily wasn't quite so sure. She knew, more so than the others, that there was a limit to Benjamin's powers. She had quizzed him, at length, about his visions. Therefore, Lily knew there wasn't much he could do to control his visions most days. They came and went like random waves trying to escape the structure of the tides.

Maybe now things would be different; maybe Benjamin did have a plan. "You're right," she said, trying to ignore her own nagging thoughts of Benjamin's visions about Jacee Trevane. "Let's not think about it tonight, let's just walk, okay?" Roy nodded, putting his muscled arm around her, as they walked on into the moonlight.

CHAPTER 17

"How dare you let her blindside me like that?" Trevane thundered. A thick vein bulged on his forehead, the one that only made its presence known when things were stressing Jacee the most.

"I was just as surprised as you," said his smug vice president of public relations. The guy had a long list of accomplishments at some of the world's most prestigious corporations, but at that exact moment all Trevane wanted to do was to fire the arrogant PR guy.

"We need to get ahead of this story. I don't want another thing mentioned about this guardian angel."

Mr. PR started to interrupt, but Trevane held up a hand. "No! I said not another word." Trevane knew what he was going to say—that the guardian angel thing would play right into their own story—but there were forces at play no one else could fully comprehend. Trevane would rather jump off a cliff than give Benjamin Dragon one second of media time. He'd been ambushed by that reporter; no blind siding would ever happen again.

"We stick to the story," he said, "The next time you set up an interview, you make sure they know that if they color outside the lines, I will never provide them another interview."

The vice president of PR nodded his understanding. At least he was smart enough to do that. "Now where are we on the spin?"

"A couple of networks have picked up the story. Two were questioning more than anything else. The other, well, they weren't quite as nice." Trevane made a give-it-to-me gesture with his hand. His vice president hesitated and then said, "I'll just say they were less than complimentary about your remarks."

"What did they say, exactly?"

Another hesitation. "I think the exact words were: 'Has Trevane found God?'"

Trevane rocked back in his chair and laughed out loud. It was the first real laugh he'd had in weeks. All those public appearances and refugee efforts required a somber attitude and he had to remind himself daily not to lose his inner optimism. After all, it was what made him a worldwide name. It was what would take him to the very top. When he finally composed himself, he saw his vice president looking at him with an uncomfortable smile. As if he didn't understand the joke. There was no joke. "Just stick to the story," Trevane ordered.

"But if you'd only tell me, Trevane," he pressed, to no avail.

Trevane interrupted, "I'll tell you what to release and when to release it and then you'll have what you need to know. Do we have an understanding?"

The vice president of PR was not used to being so controlled, and it was obvious he wasn't accustomed to being talked to like that. *Well, he'd better become accustomed to it if he wants to keep his job*, Trevane thought. "Look, like I told you when I brought you on board, I will take care of you if you help me with this. I'm sure you did your homework, and you know that the people I make promises to always come out handsomely rewarded."

Now *that* made the PR guy smile. Jacee Trevane was only one of a handful of people who could make such a promise. The PR guy knew it. "I'm sorry I doubted you," he said, happy to have regained Jacee's good graces.

Trevane gave him a curt nod of dismissal before turning his attention back to his computer. He waited for the door to close before he turned on the television as well. There were more reports of a mysterious guardian angel. There were sightings in Japan, a region where Trevane had already made modest gains and had more than a toehold. If he wanted to preserve all the gains he'd made, he needed to take action now. Trevane picked up the phone on his desk and dialed the operator. When she answered, he snapped, "Get me the president of the United States NOW!"

CHAPTER 18

Kennedy strolled the corridors of the mountain training facility. He was supposed to be giving a class teaching some young kids how to focus their mental capacity, but when they'd shown up for a lesson, he couldn't help but dismiss them. "Go have fun," he said. "Take the day to enjoy yourselves." They'd been surprised, but no one had complained.

His mind just wasn't in it today. Besides, he had learned to cherish his time. Maybe he could teach them to do the same. Who knew what was coming in their future? Who knew if they'd have such days again? So off they went as did he. They most likely headed towards the mansion's game room with its endless array of video games, movie pods, and activities geared to let their imaginations run wild. He walked deep in thought, his measured steps clumping their way down the seemingly endless corridors.

Occasionally, he would see someone who would say hello and he would merely nod. He was too tangled up in his own thoughts to stop and have a meaningful conversation with anyone. He was thinking about Benjamin again, in addition to Timothy Dragon. Kennedy knew the stresses of a wartime environment. He'd lived them too many times to count. He knew that some coped well, while others drifted into their own misery. Benjamin seemed to be taking the high road, working out his difficult emotions through actions. But Timothy was in a downward spiral, and it worried Kennedy.

He'd tried reasoning with his friend; most recently, just that morning at breakfast. Timothy had just pushed around some cereal with a spoon, never really eating, while his vacant eyes stared, unseeing, at the bowl of milk and soggy corn flakes. As with anything, Kennedy knew that resolving this dilemma would take time. How much time did they truly have though? Kennedy was a patient man, but even his self-restraint had limits. Despite his calm exterior, he was, to the core, a man of action. Seeing the reports of Benjamin traveling through the Pacific and now, reportedly, toward the United States, made Kennedy want to hop on a flight to join him.

Ah, Kennedy desired to be an adventurer again, to be out in the world instead of being relegated to cleanup work. That had been one of the most frustrating things resulting from the chaos. Jacee Trevane had taken the lead on the cleanup effort despite being behind the whole thing, ensuring that The Keepers were limited to the fringes. The role they most cherished was assisting mankind and it had been torn away from them. Now, Kennedy began to feel trapped. It wasn't the underground caves and caverns that encaged him. It was the feeling that someone else was controlling his destiny—controlling the destiny of The Keepers.

His faith was squarely with Benjamin, of that there was no doubt. He walked along for a time, trying to clear his mind, trying to think of anything but the matter at hand. Inevitably, his memories ran back to war. First, World War II, then to Korea, and finally to his secret sojourns within the Soviet

Union. Ah, how he'd had fun with those Russians—known as Soviets back then. The KGB agents were a wily bunch, but the Brits and the Americans kept them on their toes. Kennedy had always done his best to help them in any way possible. They were unaware of his hidden talents, of course, but he'd always had ways of throwing the Russkies for a loop.

He was just thinking of a time he'd watched as a KGB agent returned to his home only to find his brand new Mercedes Benz flipped onto its roof in front of his house—when the Como complex speaker system squawked overhead, "Kennedy, please report to headquarters. Kennedy, please report to headquarters." Kennedy sighed, placing a bookmark in his memory as he turned back toward the main mansion.

"I want his location verified, and I want it verified like *yesterday*," Timothy Dragon was bellowing as Kennedy entered the busy Central Security office. He watched for a moment as Timothy barked more orders in quick succession. He scanned the anxious faces of those on the receiving end of their beloved leader's wrath. They weren't used to Mr. Dragon acting in such an irrational and demeaning manner. Not that they blamed him, but there were sideways glances and looks of outright concern.

One of the things The Keepers had always tried to instill in each other was a feeling of calm. With their vast knowledge of the world, they knew that things could always be worse, and adding a high level of stress rarely made any situation better. There was a map laid out on the center table and Timothy was pointing in an erratic way from one location to another. Kennedy realized that he was mapping Benjamin's path.

"You said he was going to Hawaii. You told me that he was going to Hawaii," he reiterated.

The man next to him sputtered an excuse and received a scowl in response. He shuffled away, cowed for the time being. That was Kennedy's cue to intervene.

"What did I miss?" he asked cheerfully, sidling up next to Timothy.

Benjamin's father looked up, his face still masked in annoyance, but it softened just a bit when he saw Kennedy.

"The latest reports show Benjamin is somewhere east of California. The first indication that he was in the area was noted by witnesses in Palm Springs, but apparently he's already moved on from there."

Kennedy noted that Timothy's voice was not that of a concerned father, but of a boardroom analyst or of a Special Operations soldier, who was taking his mission very seriously—maybe too seriously. It had all the look and smell of a manhunt, and Kennedy wasn't sure he liked it.

"Is there a reason for the tracking, Timothy? Do you really think it's necessary?"

He saw Timothy's jaw clench. It was apparent the anger that had been merely simmering was reaching the boiling point. Kennedy would have to handle this situation with great caution.

"We have been through this before. Benjamin needs to be stopped. We have teams in place—one in Phoenix and one in Las Vegas. If we can triangulate where Benjamin is, there's a good chance we can stop him."

Kennedy saw the glances from around the room. He could read the vibe and it felt like a discordant note from a violin, almost a physical discomfort. There was no harmony here; they were merely obeying Timothy's commands.

"Timothy," Kennedy whispered. "I will tell you again that maybe we should see how this plays out. We should put our trust in Benjamin."

Timothy Dragon froze. His hands suddenly clenched, crumpling the edges of a large map. With a whirl, he flung the map off the table and it floated to the ground. All conversations stopped, everyone in the center quietly watched the unfolding drama. Timothy glared at Kennedy. Kennedy smiled, trying to put his friend at ease, but it didn't work.

"I called you up here to see if you would lead one of the teams to find Benjamin. Are you telling me you would refuse if I requested your help?"

"I'm here to help, although I don't see what will be accomplished if we stop Benjamin. He's helping people, for God's sake. He's doing what we all should be doing."

Then an idea struck him—the same one he'd had in the tunnels. "Yes, I think I will lead one of those parties," Kennedy said. "but not to bring him back here; I will join him. I have faith that whatever he's trying to accomplish, we will do more harm returning him here than we will standing at his side."

Timothy's face transitioned from red to a queer purple color, almost the shade of a plum.

"You will obey my orders or—"

The words stopped and Timothy's hand reached down to his side. It took Kennedy a moment to realize that the man was reaching for his phone, which had probably buzzed in his pocket. He pulled it out and looked at the screen. In a blink, his face paled, now turning a ghostly white.

"My God," Timothy whispered. "Thank you."

He fumbled with the phone as he tried to get it back into his pocket. He looked up at Kennedy, his expression confused now, like a child lost in the woods.

"I—I have to go."

Before Kennedy could ask what was wrong and what he had seen, Timothy stumbled from the room, half-running on his way somewhere, but where was he headed?

CHAPTER 19

The sun felt tantalizingly warm on Francis's pale skin. His head leaned back, his face was in full light with his eyes closed. He'd never really liked being outdoors before, but being on the edge of Lake Como, he had found something to stir his interest.

On his break, after wheeling through the cafeteria, Francis had made his way outside to the sweeping porches that overlooked the grand lake. Once he was sure he had enough sunlight, and just short of getting a slight sunburn, Francis opened his eyes and wheeled himself back toward the mansion. He was just about to reach for the door handle when it burst open and somebody swept past him. The man's movement was so forceful that it almost knocked Francis over, but the guy didn't seem to care. He was moving fast, powerfully, like he was just about to dive into the lake. Francis opened his mouth to say something, but before he could, the man rocketed into the air and was soon out of sight. It was not until then that Francis realized who the man was: it was Timothy Dragon, Benjamin's father. The guy who ran everything at the mansion.

Obviously something was wrong, and he wondered if it had something to do with Benjamin. Francis was starting to narrow down where Benjamin might be, but he hadn't told anyone. It was just a hunch for now. Better to let data compile and use it to turn fiction into fact. He was still contemplating Mr. Dragon's abrupt departure, when another familiar face came barreling down the hallway.

"Excuse me, Francis," Kennedy said, his eyes searching the area. There was concern there. "You haven't by any chance seen Timothy Dragon, have you?" So, there was something going on.

"Um, yeah, he just went out on the porch and took off."

"Do you know which way?"

"Uh, north I think. To the right."

Kennedy gave him a courteous nod of appreciation as he hurried in that direction. Francis watched him go. His curiosity was tickling the edges of his ears. Yeah, something was definitely going on. Best to get back to the computers and see if he could figure it out himself.

Kennedy braced himself against the railing and scanned the coastline. There was no sign of Timothy. There were a thousand different places he could have gone. Maybe he just needed to get away, but Kennedy sensed it was more than that. There'd been an urgency in his departure. Something had happened. Maybe he should take a stroll down to Central Security to see if they had a lead on Timothy.

Kennedy didn't know for sure, but he suspected that all the phones in possession of The Keepers were somehow being tracked. That gave him an idea. Maybe the boy, Francis, had a way of finding out where Timothy had gone. Yes, that was it. By the time he got to Central Security, Kennedy had a rough idea in mind. It was best not to tell the newest arrival all the details. It was possible he would figure things out on his own, but some things were better left unspoken.

He ignored the others as he entered the office, aiming straight for Francis.

"Did you find him?" Francis asked without looking up.

"No, but there is something I think you can help me with."

Francis swiveled his wheelchair around and looked up at Kennedy. "I'll help if I can," he said. "What do you have in mind?"

"Do we have any kind of traces on the cellphones that our teams use?" Kennedy inquired.

Francis looked uncomfortable as he looked around the room. "That's not really my areas of expertise around here, Mr. Kennedy. Maybe you should ask one of the adults about it."

Kennedy gave him a conspiratorial grin. "I'm sure it's not within your purview, but am I correct in assuming that you know pretty much everything that's going on around here?"

Francis looked uncomfortable now. "I'm not sure I—"

"Don't worry. I'm not here to make trouble. I was just hoping that you would assist me—if that wouldn't be too much of a bother."

Again Francis looked about the room, nervous. He was trying to make up his mind about whether he should break the rules or not. Kennedy explained, "It isn't that I don't trust the others in the room, but until I know what Timothy is up to, maybe it's better to keep his actions quiet."

"I'd like you to start by seeing if you can access the text logs from Mr. Dragon's phone—that and any voicemails he might have had." Francis nodded, but didn't say anything. "Second, if at all possible, I'd like you to track the phone, tell me where he is, and where he is heading. Now, do you think you could do that for me?"

In a hushed tone, Francis said, "And you're sure I won't get in trouble?"

"I promise you won't, but let's just call this a secret between you and me." Francis gave another small nod, but at least he was in.

Over an hour later, Kennedy was called back to Central Security. Francis was waiting; he still looked anxious. He waved Kennedy over to the private conference room. "What did you find?" Kennedy asked.

"So it took a little work. I had to get creative. Had to log in as some different users around here, and that might cause kind of a stink, but you said I could do it. So, after a little reprogramming and a little—I like to call it hacking—I found out all of Mr. Dragon's text logs and phone calls had been deleted."

"Could it have been done here or was that something Timothy did?"

Francis shrugged. "I honestly don't know. It could be his phone was set up that way so he can't be tracked; I'm pretty sure that if somebody here had wiped it, I would've found traces of it. They keep logs on pretty much everything."

Kennedy nodded slowly, digesting the information. "And what about the other thing? Were you able to track where the phone is?"

Now Francis smiled. "Surprisingly, that was a lot easier than the first task. I would've thought that if somebody had taken the trouble to delete all of their texts and voice records or at least protect them from being accessed, they would've disabled the phone's location services."

"And what did it tell you? Where is he going?"

Francis folded his hands in his lap, looking very studious and very proper all of a sudden. "He's going west, at least for now. The last plot I got was just west of Rome."

Kennedy nodded, deep in contemplative thought. *Where was Timothy going?* Kennedy couldn't be sure, but—well, there were so many places he could go: France, Great Britain, of course, but then there was a chance that he was making a hop over to the United States, so maybe it had something to do with Benjamin. They wouldn't know until he stopped moving.

Kennedy's attention refocused on Francis. "Thank you for your help. Is it possible to keep track of him?"

"That's no problem. I've got a program doing it, so all I have to do is check it every once in a while, and it does all the hard work. When would you like an update?"

Kennedy thought about that. He didn't want to hover, and besides he still had work to do. There were other Keepers to train. He couldn't stop that just because Timothy had flown off on a whim. "Why don't I pop in every hour or two? That is, unless you figure out something else—like if he's stopped for an extended time. Does that work for you?"

Francis gave him a thumbs-up. "No problem. I'm on it, Boss."

If this was a sign of things to come, Francis liked it. No, he didn't like it; he loved it. There was something about the intrigue, the mystery, like scattered clues you had to put together in a specific amount of time. He relished the pressure. He knew it would be a snap to track Timothy Dragon, but the one he was really focused on was Benjamin. He hadn't told Kennedy his hunch about where he thought Benjamin was headed, but on a map in Francis's head, he saw all points converging, like multiple warheads targeted at the same spot.

It would take a little more time to confirm whether his hunch was correct, but so far everything seemed to be working out beautifully. So while his fingers flew over the keyboard, and part of his mind remained focused on the task at hand, his subconscious drifted on thoughts of Timothy Dragon flying off to Portugal. Flying would be nice. Francis enjoyed it, but what he really wanted to do was walk. Now he wondered if somewhere within this mystery, within the treasures that The Keepers held, there was a way for him to see that dream become reality.

CHAPTER 20

Mrs. Birch had been saddened, but not surprised, by Roy's announcement at breakfast that he and Lily had to depart. Lily saw the look that passed between Mr. and Mrs. Birch. It was obvious how much they loved Roy and how much he loved them. She could see the pain in their eyes but she knew deep down that they would never tell him which path to take.

She respected that they were present but not overbearing. It was something that Jasmine would have found uncomfortable but something Lily felt drawn to, maybe because it was something she never had as a child. Her father, a successful surgeon, had always been working. The twins believed he felt his time was better spent in the operating room than with his twin daughters, even after his wife had died.

As they said their final good-byes, Mrs. Birch enveloped Lily in a gigantic hug. She felt like asking Roy if they could stay; they really had nowhere else to go. Without a mission or Benjamin's direction, they were really just wandering. Why not stay in Texas? Lily knew that Roy's sense of duty kept him going. How she wished Benjamin would call or that someone would tell them where he was.

That morning when she checked her laptop there had been more sightings of the guardian angel. Benjamin had made stops in Palm Springs, Las Vegas and, possibly, Phoenix. If there was a pattern, Lily couldn't see it. Media accounts were swirling now—the story was too enticing not to speculate about. A lot of airtime was given to reporters asking eyewitnesses to describe what they'd seen and experienced. What struck Lily was that the eyewitnesses never had a crazy-eyed stare or showed wide-eyed astonishment. Those touched by the guardian angel possessed a reverent calm, a deep knowledge that something had happened to them which was both holy and deserved. Almost like it was the most natural thing in the world to have been snatched away and saved from almost certain death.

There was another interesting fact: no two cases were the same. Other than the saving of lives, the events that caused the near destruction of life were never the same. Lily wondered if that was on purpose or just coincidence. In her mind she chalked it up as coincidence. Maybe Benjamin was just traveling and as he saw things happening in his mind, he just flew in at the right time to help those in dire need. Yes, that's probably what he'd been doing. She imagined him flying along, half paying attention to his path and half watching the visions in his head. Was it the same tunnel vision he'd explained to her before, or was it more broad? Was the picture going from analog to digital, from small screen to wide screen? She wished she could experience what Benjamin saw.

It was a miracle really. She'd been there when they'd all met Sibyl. While the girl had been small and gifted, there was something almost otherworldly about her. She was, after all, the last of the great Mystics. To Lily, the fact that a boy like Benjamin, who'd once been awkward and cast aside by his peers, had now been given a gift to help others was a tremendous stroke of luck, and a miracle, in and of itself. Lily felt herself being pulled to that. In that moment she knew Roy had made the right decision. They had to go. They had to find Benjamin, and they had to help him.

They decided to take a train northbound from Lubbock. They bought open-ended tickets so they could stop any time and anywhere they wanted. Sure, they could have flown, either using their own gifts or on an airplane, but Lily had never been on a real train and Roy was still deeply needed and wanted to please Lily. Besides, it would give them time to think or just sit together quietly; the train was good for that. Before meeting Benjamin and the other Keepers, Roy had never been on an airplane, but he'd always taken trains to visit family and friends, so he was well versed in the on-and-off shuffle and what happened in between. He loved the smooth thumps, the occasional whistle and rumble. Even more, he loved the look in Lily's eyes as she gazed out the window when the train pulled out of the station.

He'd really expected her to try to convince him to stay home with his parents. She'd gotten along perfectly with his mom and dad; that made his heart full and happy. He hadn't asked, but he suspected that she'd never experienced the same warmth with her family. She and Jasmine were close, and to strangers they might appear to be identical, in ways other than just their appearance, but Roy knew differently. While Jasmine could be crass and biting with her comments, Lily was sweet, thoughtful and never said an ill word without thinking it through first. Yes, he loved her.

In that moment he wondered if he was doing the right thing. It would be so easy to remain in Texas, to stay with his family and keep Lily safe. Once again, he knew that wasn't his job. His job was to help Benjamin and he thanked The Almighty with his entire soul that his Lily agreed. Off they chugged, heading north to no destination in particular, just content to be together. They were an unlikely pair thrust together by a crumbling world.

Lily was surprised to see Jasmine's name on her iPhone screen. She almost ignored the call, the fear and bitterness tasted like sour apples in her mouth. She'd been so close with her sister. They had been best friends since birth. They'd been inseparable, but recent events had shown Lily that she and Jasmine were different in so many ways. There was no ignoring it now and the distance between them only made those differences clearer. She answered the call anyway, her voice quiet yet hopeful.

"Hey, how's it going?"

The hesitancy in Jasmine's voice sent spikes of fear down Lily's arms. She tried to sound cheerful when she answered. "Oh, you know, I'm just taking the first train ride of my life."

Jasmine laughed and Lily was glad to hear the sound. "Hey, don't forget about all those times we rode the train around Disneyland. Technically, this isn't your first train ride. I get to claim that with you."

Lily returned the laugh and said, "You're right, I totally forgot about that. I do wish you were here though."

A pause hung in the air while Jasmine attempted to gather her own thoughts. Lily heard a cough on the other end. She heard muffled words which she couldn't make out; she also couldn't determine who was talking in the background. It sounded like Jasmine had covered the mouthpiece. There had never been this overt secrecy between the twins before.

Then she heard Jasmine's voice again. "Okay, give me a minute; hold on. Hey, sorry, that was Xander. You know, always being a little pushy."

"Yeah, whatever Jay Money."

Lily heard Jasmine chuckle again. She wondered how close her sister and Xander had gotten since seeing them last. Had it really been months?

"So look. We think we found something."

"Tell her the truth," Xander insisted.

"Yeah, sorry. Anyway, Xander had an idea and we thought that we would share it with you—you know—just in case he's right, which he's probably not."

"Tell me," Lily said. "What did Mr. Brainiac come up with this time?"

Jasmine laughed again but this time it was the laugh that she shared only with Lily, the one they'd tossed back and forth so many times under the sheets when their father said they were supposed to be asleep. Instead they'd had flashlights shining down on whatever funny story they had picked to read that night.

"Look, I know this may sound crazy but I think we need to listen to him this time. Xander thinks he knows where Benjamin is going."

Lily's ears perked up. "Do you mind if I put you on speaker?"

"No, go ahead."

"Okay, you're on. Repeat what you just said."

"Hey Roy, are you taking care of my sister?"

"What? Uh, yeah." Lily watched Roy's face change color; she'd call it a blush, but not to him. He'd just do it again.

"Yeah, so anyway, Xander thinks he knows where Benjamin's going."

Roy looked at Lily, hope blossoming in his eyes. "Tell us, where's he going?"

CHAPTER 21

Jacee Trevane chewed the inside of his cheek as he mulled over the news from his PR man. He unconsciously pressed a finger to the outside of his cheek, tearing the inside before realizing what he was doing. It was an old habit, a tic he had developed as a kid, most likely born out of anxiety. Maybe, in some way, this activity calmed him. It was something he'd tried to get rid of for years without much success.

His mother had first noticed it and harped ceaselessly on him to stop the activity. But it wasn't really him she was worried about. She was worried about his image and how it would affect her finances. Jacee was, first and foremost, her cash cow. "Nobody's going to sign you if you continue pursing your lips like that," she would say or, "How are they going to get a good picture if you keep chewing the inside of your mouth?" She'd always been nasty like that. She was always sweet to the producers, but caustic and rude to the sound engineers in the studio and to her son.

She'd been one of the first to go, one of his first triumphs. In the animal kingdom, some beasts ate their young. In Jacee Trevane's world, it was the other way around. He'd gotten rid of his mother. Well, he didn't do it himself, but he had his new weapon take care of the problem. The woman had become a nuisance and an obstacle to everything he had planned. He couldn't afford to have her by his side, sharing the glory and trying to tell him what to say even though he was an adult. Now she was gone and he pushed her from his mind once again and stopped gnawing on the inside of his cheek.

His timelines were all off. The carefully orchestrated story seemed to be unraveling. It took years, if not decades, to shift public opinion, but he'd done it. In five years, he'd made humanity question itself and the world around it.

Those who'd once been religious now questioned their gods. Those who had never put their faith in anything but themselves were looking for a higher being to believe in. It had been so easy to plant the stories. Global change, the proliferation of weapons of mass destruction…he'd concocted the stories himself, carefully planting seeds in the ears of reporters who had listened and then fed it back through the media.

They'd never known it was him, of course, but eventually the stories gained steam. In the beginning, he had no clue about how to choose which storyline would take hold and become the most forceful in the minds of mankind. Now two things had grabbed hold. First, that there was something happening in the universe. Whether it was created by otherworldly beings or by the world itself, to many it seemed like the world was caving in on itself. This threatened the world's population and the lives they had become accustomed to. This created uncertainty and discord.

The second, and more important thing to take hold, was fear. Like a flaming sword, fear had cut its way into the most stout of hearts. There was no escaping it. It was too real, too overwhelming.

That's exactly how he'd planned it. They'd been careful. While the damage had to be horrific, it couldn't be completely devastating. For the most part, infrastructure was left untouched. Mass hysteria would have killed everything. It would even have dashed his own hopes against the rocks, so he'd been careful orchestrating everything with surgical precision and methodical planning of each move in great detail while keeping those details to himself.

Even his closest advisors didn't know what he really had in mind. They didn't understand the weapon he had in hand, the one he'd used to shape international policy and put himself on top of the world's pedestal. It made his life and celebrity as a pop icon before look like a blip on some unknown radar station in Antarctica. Now everywhere he went, people knew him. They clamored for him; they wanted to touch him. He was adored and admired by millions.

The financial results had initially exceeded his own expectations and then continued to grow. Millions and then billions of dollars flowed into Trevane International from private citizens, corporations and even from countries. After all, why not give your money to the person who always seemed to be on the scene first? And who always seemed to have the foresight to know what the people might need? He'd personally helped stave off hysteria from rioting citizens in more than ten countries.

The leaders of those countries now owed him, but he was careful with their offerings. He could not squander what he had earned. But now things were spiraling in a different direction. He had a competitor, a nuisance: one that he thought he'd dealt with before. Benjamin Dragon was on the move, doing good wherever he touched down. Although his identity remained a mystery to the world, it's people were suddenly enamored of him, all the more, maybe, due to the mystical nature of his appearances.

Benjamin was the new flash in the pan, the guardian angel, the one looking out for the little people. Trevane couldn't understand how someone like that could take the spotlight off of himself. It was inconceivable. Jacee somehow managed to bite off a blistering rage. Suddenly, he tasted blood in his mouth. He'd bitten down too hard, too deep. His cheek was bleeding, but that woke him up.

Yes, blood was on his hands, but so what if it took some evil to attain the greater good? He saw it as a small sacrifice—the means were often justified by the end, right? He knew that if he ever told the truth, which he wouldn't, people would someday understand and forgive his actions. He had a deep faith in that fact as well as a deep faith in himself; he knew that soon the world would be unified under one leader. That leader was the man he looked at in the mirror every morning.

There was just one little flea that he had to flick from his arm: Benjamin Dragon. The boy had had his time in the sun. Jacee had given him his chance, more than one chance, but he'd stepped into the bullring now and hadn't left well enough alone. It was time to add the ultimate twist, one from which Benjamin would never emerge unscathed.

For countless days, Trevane imagined the inevitable ending. He sat back in his chair, clasped his hands behind his head, and smiled the deep, greedy smile of someone who'd just seen their ascendance to immortality.

CHAPTER 22

"Are you sure? Are you really sure?" Kennedy asked repeatedly, staring with squinted eyes at Francis's computer screen.

"Well, I guess I could be wrong, but—"

"No, of course you're right," he wavered aloud, trying to convince himself. Kennedy wasn't sure, but deep down, he knew. Francis just waited.

"Right. Thank you, Francis. I trust that you can keep this to yourself."

"Of course, but I have a favor to ask."

"Ask me; I'll do what I can. You've been quite the help, Francis."

"I was hoping I could go with you. You know, maybe I could help. I could bring a computer and still be linked up to Central Security. Who knows—you might need me."

Kennedy considered it a moment, and Francis caught him glancing down at the wheelchair. He knew what the old man was thinking. He was contemplating whether bringing Francis would be a liability—whether his extra baggage would slow his travels.

"I promise I won't get in the way and I won't slow you down. My gifts are getting stronger, and even this wheelchair can't hold me down. Please, Mr. Kennedy, I can't be stuck in this dark hole anymore. I need to get out and—well—I guess I kind of owe Benjamin, you know? I'd like to help him too, and I think the best place I can do that is with you."

The jury was out. Kennedy stared at him, his ice blue eyes doing their best to give Francis bad news, but Francis would not be put down. He was made of better stuff than that. He was strong in his own way.

"Very well," Kennedy said, "If you're coming along, I have one request as well, Francis."

"Name it, I'll do anything."

The hardness in Kennedy's eyes disappeared. A small grin crept across his face. "Call me Kennedy—no more Mister. You understand that? If we are to travel together, we must be friends." He held out his hand and Francis took it gratefully.

"It's a deal Mist—I mean, Kennedy." Man and boy smiled at each other.

Kennedy scrolled through the images on the computer screen. He had never been to the place himself, which surprised him. He loved a good tall tale, and he devoured mysteries when he wasn't training young Keepers. His favorite topics involved conspiracy theories and covered a diverse range—from the fall of Rome to the assassination of John F. Kennedy. He was spellbound by how much the public did not know, and sometimes by what they did know. It was no surprise that very few people knew the real cause of the fall of Rome. They weren't supposed to know. The Keepers had been at the center of that, for they, along with the Destructors, had been the ultimate culprits. Sometimes he wondered what the people of the world would think if they knew such a war had been waged right under their noses.

Then again, the same thing was happening now. Yes, Francis had to be right. The place made sense. It sent a message. However, Kennedy wondered uneasily if the message was sent from Benjamin or someone with evil intentions. Was Benjamin being beckoned to the place by someone with evil intent, or was he headed there of his own free will? The former frightened the old man. The last thing he wanted was for Benjamin to fly into danger. That was inevitable, really. Where wasn't there danger these days? Besides, even if the location was wrong, they would be closer to where Benjamin might end up. So that was that; off they'd go to America to find young Benjamin.

Francis didn't have a clue what to pack on this excursion because he'd never been included on a field trip before. It was obvious the laptop loaned from Central Security would come with him. He had thought he'd need to get Kennedy's help if they hadn't wanted him to take the computer. However, he didn't even need to get a supervisor to sign off. The laptop was vital in order to stay in touch with headquarters and the rest of the team, and was a critical tool to continue tracking Benjamin's flight path.

In the end, not knowing what else he would require, Francis decided on grabbing an extra set of clothes which he stuffed in the backpack strapped to the back of his wheelchair, where he could still access it.

Because the trip was so important, Francis debated whether he should leave the wheelchair behind. He'd been practicing using his own legs with the power of his mind. His legs didn't work on their own, of course; but with the unseen telekinetic energy, he was able to move them. He decided against that because he was still too awkward on his feet, and he needed to be able to concentrate on other things. He still wasn't sure if he could make himself walk in addition to focusing on people all around him. He figured that being in a wheelchair would probably help both Kennedy and him navigate with ease in the airports anyway. He was always one of the first to board a plane, and people tended to move out of his way because of his appearance. His only real concern was that he wanted to keep his promise to Kennedy: Francis would never get in the way.

"It won't be long now," Francis told himself, "before the wheelchair will be scrapped." One way or another, he would figure out how to walk. Not long ago, he talked with his computer buddy, Wally Goodfriend, also known as the most experienced Healer, about fixing his legs. Wally told him it was impossible, that nothing like it had ever been done since the old days. That last comment stuck with Francis.

If it had been done before, no matter how long ago, it could be done again. He intuitively sensed, in order to get his preferred answer, he would have to be near the source, and the best source he knew of was Benjamin Dragon. So, off they went, he and Kennedy, cruising through the airport while curious Italians stared at them as they hurried past. Francis ignored them all. He was used to the ogling. He had learned to keep his eyes straight forward.

Now he felt a new lightness that had nothing to do with the fact that he could make himself stand on his own two feet. It was like his mind had landed on the world's fluffiest pillow and was finally given a chance not to worry, but instead to yearn for something he'd never realized he needed. He maintained a vigilant hope that things were about to change and once again alter his life for the better.

CHAPTER 23

They'd been sitting in the same booth at T.G.I. Friday for the better part of three hours. Their empty plates had been removed long ago. The waitress kept coming by, giving them looks as if to say: "Are you finished yet? Can you leave?" Roy might've felt bad if Lily hadn't told him that the spot in the restaurant they'd picked provided the best Wi-Fi signal she'd found since arriving at the Atlanta airport.

The place was hopping and Lily said it was always that way, even before the destruction started. Rushing businessmen in suits hurried to grab a quick bite to eat before their flights. Displaced families sat at benches beyond the service area, looking at the food, apparently too poor to eat but too hungry not to watch. They'd somehow found enough money to make their flights, but not enough to get food. That gave Roy an idea.

He waved down the waitress. Her frown suddenly turned into a happy grin, thinking he was flagging her down to get the check. *No, not quite.* Roy had something else in mind. "May I help you, sir?" the waitress said. Her voice was thick and syrupy, as if that would get them to move from the booth faster.

"Could I put in a to-go order, please?" Roy asked. The waitress eyed him warily, like it was some sort of trick to reserve their spot longer. He wondered if the woman thought they were going to dine and dash, leaving her without payment or a tip, but that was the last thing on Roy's mind.

The waitress returned a moment later with two menus. When she left, Lily looked up from her computer and asked, "What are you doing?" Roy grinned and traced his index finger down the menu.

When the waitress returned, notepad in hand, Roy rattled off his order from memory. The waitress's narrow eyes slowly widened. When she finally had everything down, she looked at Roy and said, "Is this all for you two?"

Roy ignored the question and said, "I'd appreciate if you could put some silverware in every order." The woman nodded and slipped to the back to put in the order. Roy's grin was wide now. It was the best he'd felt in days. When the three stacks of thermal containers arrived, one carried by the waitress, and the others by two bus boys, Roy thanked them and handed over his credit card.

"We'll be keeping this table a little longer, if that's okay," Roy said. The waitress nodded in obvious agreement and went to run his card. Lily was staring at him now, her eyes twinkling with curiosity and amusement. He gave her a wink and picked up one of the container stacks, careful not to knock any knees with his oversized legs as he wound his way past other people eating in the packed restaurant.

He crossed the hallway and headed for the family who had been just short of salivating with obvious hunger. "I thought you might want a little snack," Roy said. The mother looked up, not quite as wary as the waitress had been, but still there was suspicion in her eyes, and Roy didn't blame her. "We just had some extra," Roy said in a way that would not stomp on their pride. "And, well, I thought that maybe the kids might like some. I promise I didn't take any bites." He smiled at the little girl in the second-hand dress, who looked up at him in wonder. Her brother's mouth was open and a little drool dripped out. He was hungry and the look pained Roy. "Here," Roy said, handing over the stack to the father. The man nodded, not saying a word, but Roy thought he saw the man's neck constrict, like he was choking back tears. Roy wondered if he should ask them their destination, but he thought better of it.

He returned to their table, grabbed another stack to find another family. He gave variations of explanations to the second and third families saying either, "The portions are huge; I couldn't eat it all," or "The wait time is crazy long; here's a snack to hold you over." The families appreciated the food, and he allowed them to maintain their pride. He wanted to help, not make them feel guilty for not having the means to feed their own. When he finally returned to the table, Roy found Lily with the little girl from the first family. She was giggling and Lily was smiling. Roy didn't know at what, but it didn't matter. Once again, his heart thumped with contentment. The girl smiled wide as she saw Roy approach.

"Is it okay if I ask him?" she asked Lily. Lily gave Roy a mischievous grin.

"Sure, go ahead."

Much to Roy's surprise, the little girl balled up her fists, put them on her hips and looked up at him with a serious face. She inquired, "Is it true that your ancestors were giants?"

Lily burst out laughing and that set the little girl giggling again. Roy stomped over like he was some kind of metal robot—all awkward with no joints. The little girl stiffened, but then Roy boomed, "Fee-fi-fo-fum." The words slipped away, replaced by a belly laugh that made the rest of the restaurant turn to see what the fuss was all about.

"That was really nice, what you did for them," Lily said and they waved good-bye to the little girl and her family as they left the restaurant, headed for the gates.

"I wish I could've done more," Roy answered and he really did. There were so many people in need, most much worse off than that family. They shuffled along with the snaking of the unending crowd and when they reached the right gate, Roy saw the plane was already reloading passengers.

"There they are," Lily said, pointing up ahead. It took a second before Roy saw the familiar faces of their friends. Among the crowd, Roy finally saw Jasmine and Xander. Lily hesitated for a moment, and it was Jasmine who ran to her sister first, dodging surprised passengers as she sprinted by, suddenly coming to an abrupt halt in front of Lily before enveloping her in a tight embrace.

"God, I missed you!" Jasmine exclaimed. There were tears in Lily's eyes, and Roy was happy to see the sisters reunited. Xander strolled up a moment later toting two carry-on bags.

"I don't get a hug, Roy?" Xander mocked. He was kidding, of course, but Roy gave him a bear hug as he lifted Xander completely off the ground.

"Let me down, you big oaf. Jeez." Roy set him back on the floor. Xander set down the bags and brushed himself off like he'd just been thrown into a pile of sand.

"Well, I can see that hanging out with Jasmine has helped your sense of humor," Roy teased.

"Yeah, but I'll never be a wise guy like you," Xander fired back while grinning as if to say nobody could trump that remark.

It wasn't until after Roy was behind the wheel of the rented minivan that any of them felt comfortable talking about why they'd come together. They never knew when they could be recorded by unsavory characters. Roy often wondered if their every step was being monitored. Xander was in good spirits, and that seemed to lighten the mood in the car.

As Roy pulled the van out of the parking garage, he dared to ask the question that had been formulating in his head ever since that first phone call from Jasmine: "So do you want to tell us how you figured out where Benjamin was going?" Xander shrugged next to him, like determining their friend's movements had been mere child's play.

"I don't know about you guys, but when me and Jasmine were on the road, there was a lot of time to—well—think. And surf the Internet a bunch and play games. Got to eat in some pretty cool places. But anyway, it was one night when I couldn't sleep, and I was on the Internet. And I just happened to search Google about the end of the world, or something. There was a lot of stuff, especially talking about L.A. and Tokyo and what not. But then one piece got me, something I'd never heard of. It was about a warning that had been written a few years ago. Well, I guess, maybe it's not a warning but more like rules. It's hard to explain. I mean—I'll show you when we get there.

So like, right away, I kind of put two and two together, and I figured that might be where Benjamin was going."

"Tell 'em the best part," Jasmine said from the back.

Xander nodded. "So it was just a hunch, right? Like, I read something and thought that maybe there might be a connection. But I had read a lot of things and you can put a lot of pieces together, but it doesn't always mean it's going to be a completed puzzle. Most times the pieces didn't even fit, so we just discarded them. When I pulled out the map, and I started plotting where all these people were saying that they'd seen Benjamin, you won't believe what I found!"

"What was it?" Roy asked, containing his excitement with difficulty.

"It was almost a straight line, man. Like it was an arrow pointing to where Benjamin must be headed."

"But why would he do that? Why would he be that obvious? Wouldn't Trevane and his goons pick up on that too?"

Xander nodded. "Yeah, I thought about that. But what if he *wants* to be found? What if that was his plan all along? What if he's setting a trap for Jacee? What if he finally wants to take him out, pay him back for all the bad he's done? Yeah, I think that's what it is. I think ol' Benji's got something up his sleeve that none of us ever guessed."

"But this place. I don't understand. Why would he want to go there?"

Xander looked at him, a confident grin prefacing his final statement. "Oh, you'll see when we get there, my friend. You shall see."

CHAPTER 24

She wandered around like she had when she was a young girl, aimlessly, interrupted only when drawn by the sight of a few flowers on the small hill or when a white butterfly fluttered by. She was aware of what was coming, and the only way to protect herself was to revert to her childlike self and pretend the portended time was not drawing closer. It was easier to focus on the small things: the vibrant colors of a yellow dandelion and the green clover, the smell of freshly cut grass. No one else was around, not that it would have mattered.

Her adult self might have worried for her safety, but she knew it was futile. She was bound to this place now until the events occurred as fate determined. And she knew it would happen, like all the times prior to today. The die had been cast and she'd seen it in her mind's eye. She took comfort in the knowledge this would be the last. On some level it was a huge relief.

She bent down to pick a yellow flower from its wild, unruly green field, carefully snipped off the leaves and then put it behind her ear–just like she had when she was a child. Yes, it was better this way—pretend it wasn't going to happen—transport yourself to a different place and a different time, when innocence ruled and the madness of the world had never existed.

To her surprise, her wandering finally led her to a path, and, when she looked up, she saw her final destination. *What is this place?* she wondered. Tanya Dragon gazed up at the pillars of stone, four surrounding the one in the center. It looked like books being opened for the world, and as she moved closer, she realized they were more like tablets. And then she realized, etched into each tablet, were what looked like instructions, but for whom were they intended? Her childlike self's curiosity was piqued.

Tanya wanted to see and feel the tablets. There was a language she did not understand on one. Then she turned to another and recognized Spanish. The third tablet she thought might be Russian.

Around she went until she found the tablet with her own English language chiseled into the stone. The language was plain, yet cryptic, and her wandering mind had a difficult time pinpointing what it meant. She read them, one by one—the rules—or whatever they were:

1. *Maintain humanity under 500,000,000 in perpetual balance with nature.*
2. *Guide reproduction wisely, improving fitness and diversity.*
3. *Unite humanity with a single living new language.*
4. *Rule passion, faith, tradition, and all things with tempered reason.*
5. *Protect people and nations with their laws in just courts.*

6. *Let all nations rule internally, resolving external disputes in a world court.*
7. *Avoid petty laws and useless officials.*
8. *Balance personal rights with social duties.*
9. *Prize truth, beauty and love—seeking harmony with the infinite.*
10. *Be not a cancer on the Earth. Leave room for nature. Leave room for nature.*

She read them a second time and then a third. It was like something out of a Sunday sermon. She was about to read them for the fourth time when there was a voice behind her.

"Tanya?" a voice called out to her. It was hoarse, and at first, she didn't recognize it. She turned slowly, suspicious that someone had followed her. She cocked her head to the side, her childlike mind still trying to figure out who she was looking at. "Tanya, it's me," the man repeated, and then she realized who it was, her innocence swept away by the revelation.

"Tim, you have to get out of here!" she exclaimed. "It's not safe. I—" her husband put up a hand to silence her objections.

"I know. It's okay. You don't have to be afraid, I'm here."

No. It was all wrong. He shouldn't be here. She had left in order to keep him and Benjamin safe. She was the problem. She was the plague, but it would soon end. As long as he left—he had to leave.

"Go! You have to go! I don't know when it will happen, but it's going to happen." She was crying now, the words pleading and full of the immense guilt that she constantly felt. It had taken every ounce of will she had to leave her husband. He was the only man she'd ever loved. They'd met as children and fallen in love. They shared a deep love based on mutual understanding and trust; she had broken that bond of trust. She was broken, damaged goods. That's how she felt, and that wasn't fair to him. He needed to go on with his life and not be tethered to her. She'd told him as much, but he was too stubborn to listen.

"I'm not going anywhere," he said. "I love you." He was moving closer now, and she tried to back away, but she bumped up against the stone pillar that she'd just been reading.

"No, no, no!" she sobbed. "You have to go! You have to get to safety!"

He shook his head. She could see that he was crying too, but he was smiling now. "I'm not ever leaving you again," he said. His voice was firm and resolute, but full of the love that she also felt for him.

"You don't know what you're saying. You don't understand. I'm bad. I'm wrong." She was losing herself now in his eyes, in that familiar smile and suddenly his arms were around her. And for the briefest moment, she felt safe.

Trevane watched the couple's happy reunion through high-powered binoculars. He almost felt sorry for them. Almost. It was poetic, really. He was providing them closure, like a fairytale story with the ending wrapped in a pretty velvet bow. Of course the bow would be black—black for death, but it was a pretty story nonetheless. Trevane smiled, knowing that it was only a matter of time before the son of Timothy and Tanya Dragon would appear, and then the fireworks would begin. Yes, it would be a fitting end to young Benjamin. Now all Jacee had to do was wait. The Ancient would see to tying up the loose ends.

Ah, yes—The Ancient. What a marvelous find he had been. Some would call it luck, but Trevane called it hard work. He'd followed the whispers, read the legends and put the pieces together using his contacts and his networks. The Ancient was his now, his to do with as he pleased. If there was one thing that would please him more than anything else in the world, it would be to see Benjamin Dragon buried in a shallow grave.

Elberton was ninety miles east of Atlanta. After ramming their way through the traffic moving at a snail's pace in the congested city, it still took them another two hours to reach the place. "Hey look! I think I see it," Xander said with excitement. He pointed to a structure off the highway. Roy squinted, and then he saw it too. He saw the same pillar Xander had shown him in the pictures, like an unfinished stone hut atop a hill. There were signs now informing them that the museum and the Georgia Guidestones were only minutes away.

"I'm going to park here and we can fly in," Roy said, pulling off the highway and onto a short dirt road that was probably used by cops as a speed trap. They left their belongings in the car and made their way through the woods.

"We should go first," Jasmine said, looking at Lily. Roy was about to disagree when he realized that this was indeed the best plan. The twins' knack for remaining hidden in the shadows had served them well in the past. Having them together in a lead position would help the team, but Roy still had to bite his tongue when he motioned for them to check things out. He sensed trouble ahead, and he didn't want his Lily to get there first. But there was no trouble in the forest, and when they emerged on the other side, Roy thought they were home free. As he went to say something to Lily, she put her finger to her mouth, demanding quiet.

She pointed in the direction of the Georgia Guidestones. He'd read that some people called them the American Stonehenge, although to his practiced eye and crafty hands they looked nothing like their British counterpart. Then he saw what Lily was pointing at; there were two people there, holding each other. He couldn't see who they were and thought that maybe one of them was Benjamin. Again, he wanted to say something to Lily, quietly this time, but she gave him the same gesture, this time pointing back into the trees.

"What is it?" he whispered, his mouth close to her ear. She did not answer him now. He saw the urgent look in her eyes. He knew what that meant. There was danger, and then she mouthed the name, "Trevane." They transitioned to using the rudimentary hand signals—the ones they'd practiced together for years.

"There are at least twenty," she was saying, "maybe more." Meanwhile, he wondered how she knew that much—how she'd seen them that quickly. He knew that she was right, so what were they to do? Trevane was watching the stones, along with twenty or more Destructors.

It's just the four of us, Roy thought.

Xander had obviously missed the silent conversation between Roy and Lily because he was tugging at Roy's arm now. When Roy turned to him, he saw Xander was pointing up into the air toward the clouds beyond the stones. Then Roy saw it—the familiar shape—the one he'd seen a thousand times careening out of the clouds. It was Benjamin coming, and he was quite literally flying right into a trap.

CHAPTER 25

The scene looked familiar, like he'd seen it before, and he had, of course. The Ancient had guided him. Once here, Benjamin had merely picked the path, trying to be as deliberate as he could, but as he drew closer to the stones, his throat clenched. There below him were two very familiar figures: his parents. They had never been present in his visions—it had always just been the stones. It had always looked like a happy meeting place before, and that's what Benjamin had assumed.

He hovered in the air, ripping the helmet from his head. He reached out with one hand, even as the power stream built up in his arms. They were so close. He could save them!

Then, just like in Monterey, Los Angeles and Tokyo, the ground folded in on itself, looking like the maw of some giant worm beast. They were gone in an instant. Benjamin was left with a handful of empty air and a breaking heart.

CHAPTER 26

The president didn't like hunches, but he respected them. As a military veteran of a complicated war in the Middle East, he knew that guts and gumption were sometimes all you had. He'd flown by the seat of his pants one too many times, and it seemed that since taking office that's all he had done. What he wanted now was a target. He learned that first as a linebacker at the United States Naval Academy in Annapolis. Focus your mental crosshairs on one man, and as long as your body was moving fast enough, you'd take him down. Then, during his time in the SEALs, it had been the same. Stay focused. You must stay focused.

But now the picture was blurry. Murky, like a muddy pool. They seemed to have gained a handle on the horrible destruction of cities all over the world. For some unknown reason, the United States was relatively unscathed. There had been Los Angeles, of course, and that had been the biggest blow. The economy had teetered, close to plunging over the edge. And most recently there'd been Monterey, a smaller loss to be sure, but a loss nonetheless.

The president himself had spent a wonderful two years in Monterey during postgraduate school. He remembered it fondly and knew that those memories were all that was left.

So much needless death, and for what? But then the call had come, they had chatted and after his White House secretary announced that Jacee Trevane was no longer on the line, something stirred in the president.

He replayed the conversation over and over again in his head. He knew Trevane, of course. Who didn't know the man? He'd been a savior for so many. The U.S. government had given Trevane millions for his relief efforts while some past presidents might have chosen to take that glory for themselves. This president knew that sometimes private corporations could get more done, with better end results, than the government; so he had trusted Trevane. When the call had come, he'd taken it.

The conversation had started off innocently enough. Trevane thanked the president for his ongoing support and the federal money that was funneled into Trevane International for relief efforts. They'd exchanged pleasantries. The president had promised to invite Trevane to the White House for a second time. He liked Trevane, and the icing on the cake was that his youngest daughter was home from college. He knew how much she adored the megastar. They would be surrounded by escorts at all times, of course, but he could let his daughter dream.

All of a sudden, Trevane had changed gears. His tone was the same. He wasn't one of those kiss-ups, unlike so many celebrities, and the president respected that. However, when Trevane asked the president how he would feel if all future natural disasters in cities around the world could be avoided, alarm bells clanged in the president's head.

He'd heard Trevane's interviews, of course, and wondered if he was still alluding to that spiritual current Jacee had talked about before. But, then came the kicker—the question that had put the president on his current path. Trevane had asked him, smoothly and evenly, man to man, "What if I told you, Mr. President, that if you put your faith in me, we could prevent further needless destruction?"

The president had told Trevane that he would think about it and that he would love to hear more details, but as he'd hung up the phone, something was shaken inside of him, like an early warning signal that had gone off too late. Had it been there, right before his eyes, the whole time?

He made some discreet inquiries, talked to world leaders, focusing on the ones he could trust. His questions were vague and never touched on the subject Trevane brought up, but they did paint a fuller picture of the true identity of Trevane. While it was obvious those leaders respected Trevane, it was also apparent that, on some level, they feared him. That only made the president's mounting concerns grow.

His next stop was the NSA. He'd gone straight to the top with it, not supplying a reason other than to say that he needed Trevane tracked. He also requested all relevant records from the last five years be compiled into one single report, for his eyes only. While that report would never be taken to court, it had made up the president's mind. He would need to have another conversation with Mr. Trevane, because if his current hunch was right, Trevane was a very dangerous man.

"Sir, we're five minutes out," the Black Hawk door gunner said. This flight hadn't been one of the smartest things he'd done as president, but he'd done some pretty stupid things while in the SEALs, too. His chief of staff had gone ballistic. The only way he'd been permitted to go was if he took three Secret Service agents with him, but he'd insisted all three were qualified as Special Operations, just like the rest of the men on the helicopter.

There were, of course, a number of support aircraft loitering miles away, ready to swoop in, should the president get in any trouble. As they neared the spot where the joint NSA and CIA operation had tracked Trevane, the president grinned. He was in black fatigues! It had been years, but he felt like he was home again. The smells of oil and sweat. The looks of battle-hardened men. A shiver went up his spine, not due to fear but out of excitement. Oh, how he'd missed this. Now, one way or another, he believed that he would wipe out the scourge or die trying.

Someone tapped him on the shoulder and he turned to see that it was the team commander. He hadn't given his name. "Sir, Skyhawk has visual," he said, handing the president a tablet. Skyhawk was a high-altitude drone they were using to monitor the area. Apparently, it was now on station. The operator, whoever he was, was their man with the visuals now. The president could see a couple of buildings and what looked like a small hill with something gray in the middle. Then the operator switched and the screen went to black and white. He could now see the heat signatures.

"Is that one or two signatures?" the president asked the team leader, pointing to the silver center of the picture and the man leaned in.

"I can't tell, sir. Would you like me to have him zoom in?"

"No, let's just wait."

The camera zoomed out taking in more area. There were a couple of heat signatures in the buildings, but what really caught the president's eye was the tree line. He counted the dots in his head.

"I see twenty-three," he said to the team leader. The team leader took a moment, counting.

"Respectfully, I count twenty-four, sir."

"How long until we have eyes on?" the president asked, but before the team leader could answer, the president held up his hand. Another signature had flown into the picture, too fast to be human. A bird maybe? No, too big to be a bird.

"Have him zoom in on whatever just flew into the picture," the president ordered. It took a moment for the team leader to relay the information to the drone operator, and all the while, the president stared at the screen. Something in his gut told him that it wasn't right, and his words were confirmed when the video flickered back to color and the camera zoomed in.

"It can't be," the president said, but there it was. Hovering over the sea, covering its face with its hands, facing toward must have been some kind of monument, was a person, a real human being. But how in the world was that individual staying aloft?

CHAPTER 27

"Go, go, go." His order was obeyed in silence and Trevane smirked as his troops sprang from hiding. They were just insurance, really, and they were very expendable. He might not even need them after today. Well, let them feel useful. He knew people liked that. The ace up his sleeve was The Ancient, of course, and that one had his own orders. Trevane had put safeguards in place to ensure The Ancient would do his bidding. It had been a necessary precaution. One so powerful had to be controlled. It was funny how a mind worked, how it could be twisted and played with, like malleable clay. He waited until all of his men were in place.

Benjamin was completely surrounded and Trevane only wished he could hear what the boy was thinking. "You may proceed," crackled The Ancient's voice over the radio. Trevane, of course, was the only one to hear it. It was safe for him now. He'd been in one too many close calls with Benjamin, therefore he'd taken precautions. His orders to The Ancient had been specific. "Tell me when it's safe." And he had with those three words.

Two times before he'd been cocky enough to think that he could overpower Benjamin by himself, but three strikes and you're out, as they say. This strike would *not* be against him. Trevane floated skyward, marveling at the sight before him. There was Benjamin, held in midair above the exact point where his parents had just perished. He was pinned by The Ancient in the shape of a cross, his arms stretched wide. Trevane expected to see a struggling boy as he neared, but to his surprise, Benjamin looked at ease. When Trevane neared, that look sent a tremor of doubt through Trevane, but he kicked it aside like a dented tin can, clanging away.

"So, we meet again," Trevane said grandly, like a maestro putting on a show. He even bowed and motioned to his men. "Do you like your surprise?" he asked. Benjamin didn't answer. He just stared at Trevane, unblinking. Yes, there was anger there, but not the fear Trevane had so anticipated. He wanted the boy to shake, to cry and to beg for his life, but that didn't happen. Trevane couldn't stand the suspense. "Come on. Say something, Benjamin." Then he pointed to where the monument had been, where Benjamin's parents had stood just moments before. He ribbed, "You can't tell me I'm not getting some kind of comment from your smart mouth."

Benjamin's eyes closed once, slowly, and then reopened. "What do you want?" Benjamin asked. "You've had your fun. Why don't you just kill me and get it over with? It's what you want, right? It's what you've always wanted."

Trevane shook his head in mock sadness. "I never wanted you dead, Benjamin. I just wanted you to see the light—to realize that I was right."

"Do you always rhyme when you're trying to sound cooler than you really are?"

Trevane heard someone in his ranks snicker. "Shut up," Trevane boomed.

Oh, how he wanted to tear the boy limb from limb, but he knew that whatever The Ancient had done to Benjamin, however he was holding him prevented anyone from harming him as well. It was like Benjamin had been encased in some kind of protective box of bulletproof glass. Trevane almost clicked on the radio to tell The Ancient to release him, but he thought better of that. No need to take the chance. Benjamin was his after all. Trevane bit back his mounting anger and forced a smile.

"Oh, you had your little fun playing your miracle games, but what I have in store for you will make you pray with fervor for a miracle. What I put your mother through will seem like a slap on the wrist compared to what I have planned for you." Now Benjamin's eyes narrowed with suspicion.

Trevane laughed, "You didn't know I was the one behind it? Oh, this is even better than I thought. I really thought you'd put it together."

Comprehension registered on Benjamin's face. "The doctor, the one in Switzerland, the one my mom went to. He was yours, wasn't he?"

Trevane nodded. "Was that the only part you figured out? What about your father? Did you forget about him?"

"What about him? What did you do?"

"How do you think he found his way here? I was the one who told him where to go. I was the one to tell both your parents where to go. Well, your father, directly, and your mother in a roundabout sort of way."

That had been another glorious surprise, Jacee thought. The Ancient was no one- trick pony. The most powerful gifted person Trevane had ever heard of, also had limited powers of telepathy, so once Benjamin's mother's wires had been scrambled, it was easy for The Ancient to implant certain visions and precise destinations. That's how she had always ended up in the right place at the right time. Or wrong, depending on how you looked at it.

"And what about the rest of it? Why did you do it? Why did you kill all those innocent people?"

Trevane tensed. This was not where he wanted the conversation to go. No one knew his secret. No one knew who The Ancient really was. He'd always known that mass murder was the last resort and that many of his followers, gifted or not, would never understand. That's why he'd never told them.

Jacee lied, "We both know it was your mother, Benjamin. Somehow, through whatever that doctor—who I disposed of by the way—did to her, your mother acquired a deeper understanding of her gifts. In essence, she became the strongest of us. Stronger even than you. I can't believe you don't want to own up to that."

"You're a liar. She never did any of it, and you know it."

"Well, I guess we'll never know, will we?" He glanced down at the ground, where the two elder Dragons had been buried. Benjamin's eyes scanned the rest of Trevane's Destructors.

"Can't you see what he's done? Can't you see that he's been killing innocent people? I don't know what he's promised you, but he's lied to you. He's lied to all of us. In fact, he's deceived the world and, what's worse, he believes that what he's done is right."

"That's enough," Trevane snapped, quieting the murmurs within his ranks.

Maybe he should have The Ancient kill them all, just to stave off any uncomfortable conversations in the future. His secret had been his alone, up to that point. He wondered how Benjamin suspected—how he apparently knew—that his mother wasn't the one. The same fear he'd felt before gripped his chest suddenly when he realized the truth. Trevane had had The Ancient relay similar visions to Benjamin and his mother. Somehow this had opened up a separate link which allowed Benjamin to figure out the messages weren't coming from his mother but from another. Trevane couldn't take the chance that what Benjamin knew could become public. As discreetly as possible, Trevane depressed the call button on his radio.

CHAPTER 28

The team on the ground had gotten the directional mic set up in the nick of time. The president heard the entire thing. In his mind, there was no doubt, although he knew others would question his decision later.

The president patted the man next to him on the shoulder and commanded through his headset mic, "Take the shot, son."

The man nodded, rested his cheek just behind the rifle sight and pulled the trigger.

Roy hadn't heard a lick of the conversation between Trevane and Benjamin, but he'd felt the tension mount, had watched their body language, and knew that—despite the fact that there were only four of them against twenty-four opponents—he had to do something. So he'd given the signal. Although they were four against an overwhelming number, they had love and friendship on their side—love for one another and love for Benjamin. The others trusted him, and they were determined not to let him down. Roy counted down in his head: *Five, four, three, two*, but just before the one clicked over, he heard a shot in the distance.

In a split second, he knew what it meant. He knew someone would die, and his heart cracked as his eyes went wide, fully expecting Benjamin to fall to the ground, but it wasn't Benjamin. It was Trevane. Like a rag doll, he was cast to the ground, where he landed with a dull thud. Following that was complete silence. Roy sensed the shock rippling through Trevane's ranks. He took advantage of this, and he didn't hesitate. "Let's go," he ordered, and the four darted into the air.

The Black Hawk howled in over the trees, thumping its way to the objective. The president couldn't see because he wasn't in the cockpit, but he was still watching the Skyhawk feed, and he saw Trevane's body come to rest on the rubble below. He breathed a sigh of relief, praying that he'd made the right decision. His men were ready to take out the rest, if necessary, and guns bristled dangerously from both sides of the Black Hawk. The sniper who'd taken out Trevane retained his spot next to the president. For a beat, the president considered grabbing one of the man's weapons. He was trained—of course—well-trained, but he had promised he wouldn't go maverick with the exception of an emergency. However, it seemed that his men had things well in hand, but as they thundered closer, his eyes went wide again.

Faster than his own chariot, four objects rocketed into view, entering through a quarter of the circle of Trevane's men. He saw the rest turn but he was unsure if they were turning because of the sound of the Black Hawk or due to the sudden disappearance of their companions. A moment later the same thing happened again. Half were gone, but where?

Then came the most incredible. The rest scattered, flying off in pairs, leaving the president with another difficult decision to make.

"Get ready to take them all," he said through the radio. He could see it himself now. They were coming in hot, so close, and the president wondered if it would be smarter to wait for answers or just make the decision now—deal with the threat. He had no idea who or what the other four had been, but he knew if they had anything to do with Trevane, they could be and probably were just as dangerous as the dead megastar. Yes, it would be better to make that call—to get it done—so they swooped in, and the president made his decision.

CHAPTER 29

The Black Hawk came to rest like it had settled on a pile of fluffy snow. The pilot was good. The president would have to thank him; in fact, he would have to thank them all—if they got out alive. He was taking a big risk, quite possibly the biggest gamble of his life. But if his dad had taught him one thing, it was that you never got ahead in life without taking a few risks. The president was about to jump to the ground when the team leader grabbed him, "Sir, you can't go out there."

"Look, I'm going out there, and you're welcome to come with me, but you saw the same thing I did, and I don't believe these people mean us any harm."

"But, sir—"

"You've got fifteen seconds to secure the perimeter before I step out, got it?"

The president saw the warrior's jaw clench, but he nodded. Another good man. *One Mississippi, two Mississippi, three Mississippi*—The Special Operations soldiers (the president suspected they were Delta Force), rushed out as he continued to count down under his breath. By the time he reached fifteen Mississippi, they had established a hasty perimeter and were now surrounding five figures, not including the lifeless body of Jacee Trevane on the ground.

The President of the United States exited the aircraft feeling wary, yet optimistic. His confidence waned when he got his first really good luck at the five figures. They were just kids, barely even teenagers. The few questions he'd had a chance to actually concoct in his head now fluttered away. *Teenagers?*

One boy was tall, and the president thought he was probably bigger than the men he'd just flown in on the helicopter with. He cut an impressive figure, but the president could see he was still just a child. Another boy, lanky with scruffy hair, stood there grinning. It was as if he thought the trouble they'd just gotten into was the funniest thing he'd ever done in his life. There were two Asian girls; it was obvious they were identical twins, although one wore a purple streak in her hair while the other had a white streak. They stood staring at him, unafraid. The president might have assumed the big one was their leader, but then he saw the fifth.

The president had met all sorts of leaders in his time, both during his service in the military and inside the halls of government. He had developed a keen eye for distinguishing those most fitting in positions of command. This last teenager—a boy who might have weighed a hundred twenty pounds soaking wet and with barely a hint of puberty—drew the president's undivided attention.

He was drawn to the boy's sense of calm. No, not calm—serenity. It was not in that New Age "Hey, come and share a drink of herb tea with me" kind of way, but in a way the president thought he projected himself. It was the demeanor of quiet confidence in himself, harboring no secrets. In many ways, as the president looked at this boy who met his gaze earnestly, he felt like he was looking into a mirror, looking at a reflection of his younger self. Yet the president knew that at that young age, even he hadn't had the same unspoken confidence that this teenager possessed.

"Hello, Mr. President," the boy said, "I was hoping we could talk alone, if that's okay with these gentlemen."

Wow, the kid had nerve! But it wasn't an order and the president knew that. The president cleared his throat. "First, can you confirm if I made the correct call?" The president glanced at the body of Jacee Trevane, whose lifeless eyes stared off into oblivion.

"Yes," the boy said, "you made the right call, Mr. President."

The president grunted. His hunch had been right. For some reason—and he knew his closest advisors would think he was crazy—he wanted to trust this boy. He announced, "I'll give you five minutes." Oh, how his black-clad warriors stiffened then. "It's okay," the president assured them, "I'll be fine."

The boy acknowledged the warriors and walked outside the perimeter while the president followed him. "Oh, and have them turn the mic off, if you don't mind," the president ordered over his shoulder. Better to talk privately. Who knew what this boy was going to say?

When they were safely out of earshot, the kid turned toward him. He held out his hand and said, "Mr. President, my name is Benjamin Dragon." The president shook the boy's hand; it was a firm handshake.

"I'm sure you have questions, Mr. President. I can't promise to answer them all, but I'll answer the ones that I can."

The president wasn't sure whether he liked the sound of that. He needed answers. His country and the world needed answers, so he went straight to the heart of it. There was no sense in wimping out now.

"Trevane—was he the one behind it?"

"Yes, Mr. President."

"And how did he do it? No weapon on Earth could do what they did. I have to answer to a lot of people who deserve to know what happened. Religious zealots call me every day, and the environmentalists believe the United States has killed the world. How do I explain this to them?"

Benjamin nodded his understanding, like a sage master considering a grave request. "As I'm sure you've seen, Mr. President, my people have a certain array of gifts, or powers, if you will. One of those gifts allowed Jacee to do what he did."

"You're saying now that he's dead the threat is gone?"

The boy nodded. "As far as I know, he was the only one to possess that power."

"You said your people—you said you have gifts, superpowers. Are you from here or are you from another world like Superman or something?" The question sounded absurd coming out of his usually very articulate mouth.

"Mr. President, we're from Earth, born and bred here just like you. To further put your mind at ease, yes, Jacee was one of our people. Some countries are benevolent and they extend their goodwill to those in need, while other countries seem to wreak mayhem upon their own and are dead set on expanding their control over other countries. Just like countries, we've had both good and bad in our own history. My kind are called The Keepers, while the less benevolent are called The Destructors."

"These Destructors—there must be more of them. What's to keep them from picking up where Trevane left off, Benjamin?"

"I can't be sure, of course, but I can say that Jacee was the mastermind. He was the one that rallied The Destructors together, and without him, they're lost. I'm sure they'll either come to us begging for forgiveness, or they'll skulk off to hide. I can promise you the ones who made trouble will be found. We will find them and bring them to justice."

The president shook his head, trying to understand. He'd never been briefed on any sort of cross-civilization. Yet he found himself wanting and needing to know who they were so he asked, "You say you're called The Keepers. Why? Help me understand. What is it that you do?"

Benjamin smiled, for the first time looking shy—looking his age. "For thousands of years, The Keepers helped guide civilization. We were instrumental in helping mankind understand the world around them. We served as advisors, trying to propel them in the proper directions. We took that role very seriously, until around two thousand years ago when it all changed. Mankind said it no longer needed us, and there was a war between our people—just like the one you've witnessed first-hand. But we won, and now it's time, Mr. President; we're ready to help again."

The president's eyes were wide now, "You're saying you're going to go public? You're going to tell people that you exist? Well that's—I don't—"

"That's not exactly what I meant, Mr. President. I agree with you. If most people knew about us, they would either try to worship or kill us. Jacee wanted to rule the world. He wanted to be worshipped and have the world see him as their savior. That is NOT what we want. We know there are leaders, like you, who want to help their people. Your goal, as well as that of your counterparts', is to make the world better, and we have the gifts to help you make that happen. There are those within The Keeper family with gifts like the ones you've seen today. There are others endowed with the power of healing. That, in and of itself, could help many. Then there are the kindest of our people, The Growers. They are endowed with the ability to make an acre of cornfields with one single kernel of corn. Imagine what that can do for our world, Mr. President. Imagine how many people we could help."

"You're saying that your kind will allow me to use them to accomplish this?"

"Consider it a collaboration, Mr. President. Imagine the calamities that could result if control of The Keepers, Healers and Growers fell into the wrong person's hands. No, we will not be used, but we will provide assistance. We're happy to do so, with our only request being that our presence remain a secret. We would need you to make us a solemn promise that you would maintain our anonymity."

It all sounded too good to be true, like a gift dropped down from the heavens. Doubt once again crept into the president's thoughts. He needed assurances and promises as well, but what could this kid give him to help him understand and provide an unparalleled trust? No, that was impossible.

As if the boy had read his mind, he said, "Mr. President, what if I could show you that we're the good guys? That just like you, we want the best for the human race."

"I don't know how you could make that happen. Benjamin, I'm sorry. I really do want to believe you, but—"

Benjamin nodded. "Here, Mr. President, let me show you we are deserving of your trust."

The president heard a sucking sound, like he'd been flushed down a toilet, and then shoved down some watery tube. His vision went dark, and he felt like he might fall. Within moments it cleared, but he no longer saw Benjamin.

"Sweet Jesus," he muttered as the images flew by, one after another. They were just snapshots. For some reason he suddenly comprehended the entire story behind the slideshow—what had transpired and what had been said.

It was impossible, yet he began to understand. His body relaxed while he watched ten thousand years' worth of photographs play in front of him like a picture show. It was the most confounding, awe-inspiring photo album the president, or maybe anyone, would ever see. When he came to, Benjamin was waiting with a knowing smile, "Pretty amazing, isn't it?" Benjamin asked.

"Yeah," the president answered, his voice hoarse. He tried to swallow but found that his mouth was parched and his throat dry, but other than that, he felt more at ease than any time in recent memory. "Okay, Benjamin. You've got yourself a deal."

EPILOGUE

After the president convinced his men that we weren't a national security risk, we shook hands one last time, and I promised him I'd be in touch soon. *Weird, huh?* Me, a fifteen-year-old kid with the president's phone number, but I promise he won't be the last. There were other world leaders I'd have to meet, but there was no time for that now. Once we were sure everyone was gone, I led my friends to the shack a half mile from where the monument had stood and where my parents were now buried.

Along the way, Kennedy and Francis showed up, floating down from the clouds. Kennedy wore his typical knowing grin.

Francis asked, "Aw man, did we miss the fight?"

I ignored the question and quietly told them about my parents. Kennedy bowed his head.

"I'm so sorry, Benjamin," he said.

Francis was quiet for the first time since I'd met him. I even saw a glint of wetness in his eyes. I nodded my silent thanks, and led my family on, closer to the answer.

The shack was where we found him. I'm not really sure what I was expecting. Maybe someone who looked like a vampire preserved way past their life expectancy. Instead, we found a kid who looked a lot like me. But his eyes—yeah—his eyes, that's what gave him the appearance of an old sage.

He'd seen so much, maybe too much. There was an additional surprise because surrounding The Ancient were four women who straight off I knew were sisters. The Ancient introduced us to The Four Sisters. "They are Healers," he said in the same voice I'd heard in my head.

I felt like I knew him by now, but I really didn't. "Are they the ones that kept you alive?" I asked, my curiosity getting the better of me. Just like the president had wanted to comprehend matters unknown to him, I too felt a need to understand.

The Ancient nodded, "They and myself. The Four Sisters have wondrous gifts which we hope to teach you soon."

Another vision flashed in my head, imported by The Ancient. It showed the five of them during ancient times, splashing in some river, which I knew intuitively was the Nile. The Four Sisters had happened upon The Ancient, much like Moses had been found by Pharaoh's sister. They'd loved and raised him, promising him that he'd never grow old. So they'd hidden for what must have seemed like forever as they watched civilization flow all around them. During all that time, they'd never once been discovered until bad luck caught up with them.

The Ancient showed me, via images, the unfortunate events that had unfolded. One of The Sisters had gone half mad, and she had sought out the help of a prominent psychologist; it was the same psychologist my mom had seen, the one with ties to Jacee.

My mom—The story reminded me that my mom was dead. Now that the chaos of the previous fight had subsided, I suddenly remembered she was dead. The overwhelming pain stabbed me with an intensity I'd never before experienced.

I'd been strong and taken on the role of adult when I was needed. But now I was just a kid again, and all I wanted to do was crumble in a corner to cry and mourn my loss.

But then The Ancient smiled and stepped closer to me to grab my hand. "Come," he said, "I have something important to show you."

We walked back up the hill to my parents' last resting place. I didn't want to go, but I didn't resist as he pulled me farther and farther. When we were twenty paces from where the monument used to be, he stopped and pointed. I forced myself to look. Jacee's body was gone; the president's men had seen to that. But I didn't want to look at my parents' graves. I already felt unable to function due to my grief. But I looked anyway, one more time, and that's when I saw it. The rough mound had changed. There was a square indentation at the top.

I let go of The Ancient's hand and walked forward, my legs shaking. I felt like a newborn calf standing up for the first time – uncertain, legs trembling and a bit clumsy. However, I did get to the square stone slab laying on the ground. I looked back with apprehension at The Ancient, and he said, "Lift it." So I moved it aside with my mind, anxious now. Once the lid had been removed, I rushed to the opening. There was a hole, and when I peered inside, my breath caught.

"Who's there?" my dad asked, shielding his eyes from the sudden bright sunlight.

"Mom! Dad! It's me!" I said with growing excitement. I lifted them out of the hole. They were covered in dirt and grime, but I didn't care. I couldn't believe my eyes; they were alive. The Ancient had protected my parents from The Destructors. Almost bowling them over, I ran to them. Once again, we were together.

No story is ever really finished. Take me, for example. After we left Georgia, we went home to Italy. I had my parents back again, and at long last my mom was getting the medical help she really needed. Finally, she was getting better. The Ancient and The Four Sisters came with us, promising to teach us everything they knew. That's what my trip had been—a test of fortitude and trustworthiness. The Ancient wanted to know if I could be trusted with the knowledge he possessed. Part of what he'd shown me, I had shared with the president.

So now it was my responsibility but, through this trial, I had been reminded I was not in this alone. I had the help of Roy, Lily, Jasmine and Xander. Then there was Francis. I hadn't really liked that kid from the start. But it turns out, he's a pretty good guy. The Four Sisters even think they might be able to help him recover the full function of his legs. I can't tell you how good that makes me feel.

Well, I'm off now. The president's going to introduce me to the prime minister of Great Britain. It's all super hush hush, of course. Roy and the others insisted on joining me, and I wouldn't have it any other way.

So now I'll leave you because my friends and I need to keep the world safe. Please keep in mind, if you ever see a dark speck in the sky or if you hear a weird story that sounds like it's better suited for the movies, know that it just might be us.

We're always here, and we're always watching.

I hope you've enjoyed this story.
If you did, please take a moment to write an honest review. Even the short ones help. Your reviews fuel this book's success and are much appreciated.

TO GET A FREE COPY OF ANY C. G. COOPER NOVEL AND HEAR ABOUT NEW RELEASES VISIT:
>> http://CG-COOPER.COM <<

More thanks to my Beta Readers:
Fran, Jeff, Don, Jim, Glenda, Susan, Kathryn and Cara:
Thanks for helping to bring my crazy ideas to fruition.

Made in the USA
San Bernardino, CA
28 March 2019